WILD CARDS

The Second Virago Anthology of Writing Women

edited by
Andrea Badenoch
Maggie Hannan
Pippa Little
Debbie Taylor

A *Virago* Book

Published by Virago Press 1999

This collection and introduction copyright © Andrea
Badenoch, Maggie Hannan, Pippa Little and Debbie Taylor

Writing Women is supported by

Acknowledgements are due to the editors of the following publications
in which some of the poems first appeared: Acorn Dublin Writers
Workshop 1993, *The Honest Ulsterman, Krino, London Magazine,
Probably Dreaming* (Broadwords/Waldean Press, 1997), *Sending Messages*
(Opera North in association with Sunderland Leisure Libraries and
Arts), *Seneca Review, Smith/Doorstep, Steeple* 2, *The Stinging Fly, Stride,*
10 *Poems* (Redstone Press, 1993).

A CIP catalogue record for this book is
available from the British Library

ISBN 1 86049 548 6

Typeset in Novarese by M Rules
Printed and bound in Great Britain by CPD Wales

Virago Press
A Division of
Little, Brown and Company (UK)
Brettenham House
Lancaster Place
London WC2E 7EN

Contents

Contents

Poetry editors

Maggie Hannan lives in Hull, where she studied Philosophy She has worked as a stonemason, professional life model and cleaner to subsidise her writing. She won a Gregory Award in 1990 and her first collection 'Liar, Jones' (1995 Bloodaxe) was shortlisted for the Forward Prize for Best First Collection. She worked as Writer in Residence at the University of Northumbria in Newcastle, and received a K. Blundell award in 1997. She currently works in a bookshop.

Pippa Little lives in Northumbria and has three children and a doctorate in women's poetry. Her writing career began in print journalism in Scotland where she won a Young Scots Poet award and a Gregory Award for her poetry. She now teaches creative writing and literature in Newcastle upon Tyne at the university and in adult education. Her poems have appeared in every major poetry journal.

Prose editors

Andrea Badenoch lives in Newcastle upon Tyne with her three children. Her first thriller *Mortal* appeared in 1998 and was described as 'a first-rate first novel' and 'grim, beautifully written and in many ways profound'. Her second book *Driven*, about car crime and homelessness is forthcoming from Macmillan. She now writes full time.

Debbie Taylor lives in Newcastle upon Tyne and has one child and a PhD in Psychology. After two years living in a traditional African village, she returned to England to become Editor of the award-winning *New Internationalist* magazine. Her fourth book of non-fiction, *My Children, My Gold*, Virago 1994, was shortlisted for the Fawcett Prize for women's writing. She currently edits *Mslexia*, the new national magazine for women writers launched in March 1999.

Introduction

This is the second Writing Women/Virago Press anthology, in what has become an annual project. Again, thousands of submissions were received and *Wild Cards* represents some of the best of new writing. As with the first anthology, *The Nerve*, there is work from all parts of the United Kingdom and beyond and the contributors range in age from those in their early twenties to those in their fifties. Again we have an equal number of prose writers and poets.

The work here has both substance and style. *Wild Cards* contains poems and stories which address the broad cultural concerns of race, class, family, sex and sexuality, but with the focus firmly on individual experience. There is a strong imaginative quality to much of the writing, the effect of which is often unsettling. It is characteristic of the writers represented here that the uniqueness of voice which each has achieved is matched by an idiosyncratic response to the everyday and the ordinary.

We believe this second anthology will be as successful as

the first, introducing new writing to readers and publishers, as well as confirming the value of women-only collections. *Wild Cards* offers writing which is sharp, witty and tender, but above all, fully engaged with the experience of living and writing at the beginning of a new century.

FERNE ARFIN

You can keep the dog

Barry Jackson had a hearts and flowers tattoo above his left wrist. He'd had it done at a carnival after a Fourth of July picnic during which he was in charge of the beer. His initial and Sheila's were in the middle of the heart: B and S. He told Sheila that being tattooed had hurt a lot. It was a declaration of love, he said, so that she would accept his proposal. Sheila told him she thought it was romantic.

Years later, when Barry told Sheila he was leaving her for Sandra, she said, 'At least you won't have to change the tattoo.'

'Don't you *ever* run out of mouth?'

'I always knew it really meant bullshit,' Sheila said.

Barry leaned on the railing, studying the porch floor with such intensity that, instinctively, Sheila looked down as well. When they both looked up, their eyes met. Barry's were wet and sorry.

'I'm tired. I'm going now,' he said, but the porch held his boots like mud.

'How long, you suppose, before you get tired of her too? Bored?'

'I'm not bored with you Sheila. I'm just . . . I'm . . . Oh, forget it.'

'You think this is some kind of movie? *So long sweetheart: forget it?*'

'Dammit, Sheila, I'm exhausted. You wear me out, that's all . . . She doesn't expect so much.'

'So much what?'

'I gotta go.'

Sheila blocked his way. 'So much what?' she said.

'I don't know. Nothing . . . everything . . . you just . . . God, Sheila, you're just too greedy. You want too much from me.'

'Greedy? I*m* greedy? For what? A little talk, maybe? A smile? A chance, once in a while to eat somebody else's cooking? From where I'm looking I don't see that I needed more than one bed at the same time.'

'All right. Enough.'

'Not till you tell me.'

Barry stared at her. 'You just don't get it, do you?' he said. 'You never stop . . . It's never . . . good enough . . . always something . . . something . . . Hell, it's not like you haven't said so yourself.'

'People say things when they're angry. It doesn't mean anything.'

'Yeah, well. Whatever it is you want, Sheila, I haven't got it any more. Maybe I never did.'

'Yeah, maybe,' Sheila said.

Before she went inside, Sheila watched Barry load the last of his boxes into the back of the Camarro. He untied his mangy yellow dog from the gatepost. The dog pranced and bounced, yelping when his tail whipped through the firethorn bush at the bottom of the path.

The roast she had thawed for supper was sitting on the counter in a pool of blood. She threw it out and began to mop up the blood with a sponge. Dry-eyed in the kitchen, she rubbed the sponge back and forth, back and forth, harder and harder. She scrubbed furiously, squeezing the sponge so tight that the backs of her fingers scraped the scratched Formica, startling her back into the moment, trembling, puzzled.

She lifted the receiver of the kitchen phone, stood holding it a moment as if trying to decide who to call, then lowered it. She put the kettle on for coffee, but when it whistled she lit a cigarette and went to take a bath.

He had cleared out his things while she was at work. Not a sign of him was left. Not a toothbrush, not a packet of razor blades. She opened the medicine cabinet. He'd even bothered to take the fancy deodorant gel he'd been using lately.

Sheila climbed into water as hot as she could stand, sat back and inhaled steam. Eyes closed, she ran her finger along the edge of the tub. She traced idle circles on the steamy ceramic tiles until her fingernail caught in the one that was cracked. He'd left it that way when he'd put them up. 'It'll do the job,' he had said when she had complained that he was useless at handyman things.

She sat up and wiped the tile clean. A bit of grout, where he had tried to seal it, came loose and scratched against the flat of her hand. She rolled it between her fingers, considering it, first this way, then that. She sat forward, her elbows propped on her pulled-up knees and held the bit of hard plaster close to her face. Her brow creased, she examined it, turning it between her fingers as though she were looking for a flaw in a precious stone, as though the thing held a most important secret. She closed her fist around it and dropped her head on her knees.

After a while she went to bed, the evening sun still beating against the window shades, the bit of plaster still clutched in her hand.

The next day, when she got home from work, Barry's yellow dog was waiting for her, tied to the porch railings with a piece of rope. There was a note taped to the screen door in Barry's hand. 'You can keep the dog,' it said. 'Sandra's allergic.' He hadn't even bothered to sign it.

She crumpled the note, untied the dog and patted its head. 'Hey, dog,' she said. 'You might as well come inside.'

She went straight to the kitchen. She had rolled up her sleeves, tied on an apron and thrown open the fridge before she remembered that she didn't have to cook Barry's dinner. Anyway, she hadn't bothered to take anything out of the freezer so there was nothing to cook. The entire contents of the refrigerator consisted of a Tupperware pitcher of orange juice, an onion and a tired-looking block of store cheese.

There was vodka in the freezer. She poured two fingers of it into a glass, considered this, then poured another two and coloured the vodka with a little orange juice.

The dog followed her into the living room. He circled the rug, chose a spot in the middle of it, sat up and stared at Sheila. She raised her glass to him. 'Hey, dog. Here's to us.' The dog cocked his head. His tail swept the rug two or three times. He watched Sheila drink. She could see his wet brown eyes fixed on hers through the bottom of the glass. Every time she lowered the glass, he lifted his ears and came to attention.

'You know, people don't like to be stared at,' she said. 'You could get arrested.' At the sound of her voice, the dog's tail was in motion again. She frowned. 'Food?' she said. 'Suppertime?' The dog leapt up and raced for the kitchen.

Sheila wrinkled her nose as she spooned the livery slop out of the can. The dog jumped around in a frenzy. His snout was in the dish before it hit the floor.

'You're easy to please.'

He wasn't. She'd no sooner sat down with another couple of fingers of vodka – this time she'd skipped the orange juice – than he was at her side, snuffling and pushing his greasy, wet nose under her hand. 'What? . . . *What?*'

She checked that his water bowl was full. 'You're OK,' she said. 'Settle down.'

The dog curled up on the rug and groaned. Every time she moved, he raised his head to watch her. To avoid his gaze, unmediated by tact, she flicked on the television and surfed channels with the remote control.

On a comedy show, pretty women complained they couldn't find men. 'Right,' Sheila said. She pressed the advance button. There was a chat show, where a pair of café waitresses, with hair like Loretta Lynn and Tammy Wynette, argued across a sheepish-looking man wedged between them, who might have been their boss, while the hostess whipped the audience into a gladiatorial frenzy. *Fire 'em both!* they shouted. *Make 'em mud wrestle! Are you a man or a mouse?* On another channel, a congressman worried about the future of food stamps. She held down the advance button with her thumb and unfocused her eyes as the channels whipped by, blips of sound and colour.

Meanwhile the dog had weaselled his head under her hand and was demanding attention. Sheila patted him once or twice, then shoved him away. 'Enough,' she said. 'Get down.' He skulked over to the far end of the couch and dug himself in, facing her.

Raising her glass, Sheila found it was empty. She snapped off the television and got up to pour herself another. Before she returned to the living room, she went through the house turning on lights, one room after another, trying to open up the tight spaces with light. The kitchen, the bathroom, the bedroom that always looked shabby, no matter how many magazine pictures she tried to copy, the spare bedroom, never any use except when she or Barry set up the camp-cot after a fight.

Back in the living room, the dog had settled himself in the spot she had warmed, so she sat on the floor, her back against the couch. The dog, perhaps thinking this was a game, jumped into her lap, whipping his tail across her face and spilling her drink.

'Jesus Christ. Get off me!' she shouted.

The dog dropped his head and meandered over to his favourite spot, in the middle of the rug. There he sat, panting, watchful. The panting pitched up into a whimper that gradually became an insistent whine, like a frightened child.

'Oh God,' Sheila said. 'What do you want from me? Can't you stop? Can't you stop?' Then she wiped her eyes.

MARION MATHIEU

He remembers

the butcher shop in Harlem,
rabbits strung round a barrel by their ears,

his old man cursing in French,
gulping down oysters and whiskey at the kitchen table,

his mother staring into the sink,
asking a drowned Irish boy the price of potatoes,

his sister bobbing her hair,
sneaking out to meet an Italian bookie,

his favourite aunt
dancing off the edge of the fire escape,

his old man
bursting a blood vessel in his brain,

his mother
being strapped into a bed at Bellevue,

his bow-legged brother whispering in the dark,
what do you think they'll do with us?,

a man called George George
handing him a tiny metal car.

Yet when he wakes up hollering
the nightmare's always the same,

just some guy
coming through the window to get him.

In accordance with his wishes

his ashes travelled upstate
to a town he'd never visited
and spent the day
with a puzzled but obliging volunteer fire department,

the proceeds from the sale of his record collection
were donated to the Harlem Boys' Choir,

and his paintings were scattered across the city
by a forty-something housewife from Scarsdale,
who'd promised to wrap them round lampposts,
stuff them through letterboxes,
or toss them over her impeccably groomed shoulder
and never look back.

No one could remember him knowing this woman
or having a special fondness for firemen,
black boy sopranos,
or the suburbs,

and we were left wondering about the probable fate
of six hundred and thirty-seven small canvas rectangles,
each one depicting a single moment
in the final hours

of a crew of naked, balding, pot-bellied men,
as they strap themselves to masts,
cling to the backs of sea serpents,
or struggle into tiny leather boats.

The accident

We were hurtling over a bridge,
directly into the path of an oncoming lorry,
when we saw it.
We shouted for Mother to stop.

She hollered back, shut up you kids,
I can *see* the damn lorry.
No, we said, the *duck pond*.

Mother swore under her breath.
The car skidded off the road.
We jumped out and ran towards the pond,
where a large white drake
with a paper crown on his head
was holding court.
Mother followed with the picnic basket.

Fuzzy princelings nibbled at her ankles,
hoping for a snack.
Mother stepped on one.
We gathered round the tiny heap of feathers,
willing it to get up.
The duckling staggered to its feet,
faltered, fell, died.

Mother screamed, I've got it on my shoe,
it's all over my *shoe*!
We slid off her sandal, wiped it on the grass,
reassured her
that these things happen.

The drake stared at us in silence.
It started to rain.
We climbed back into the car,
ate our sandwiches, drank our lemonade,
sang all the way home.

The gin and tonic lady

mixes another drink
slides a monkey grin
across her freckled face.

A Great Dane
the size of a horse
jumps up on the bed,
buries its head in my lap.

She coughs, lights up a cigarette,
peers at me
maliciously
through a cloud of smoke.

Now *really*.

Don't tell me
you don't like *dogs*,
either.

The attendant

I've peeled my clothes away and they lie folded beside me,
shrouds for a large virgin. Dressed, in fabrics which float in an
obscure outline around me, I can kid myself. In my swimming
costume I can't pretend any more that what I am isn't visible to
the world.

A woman on a bench at the other side of the changing
rooms looks at me. She's too fascinated to shield me from her
rudeness, even when I meet her eye. The woman who attends
to the swimming baths sweeps water towards a drain. She does
it slowly, there's no rush. Her nonchalance is comforting. It
tells me she's seen it all before. There are other people like me.

It's some time before I brave the exposure of the pool. I've
come early, to the early bird session, to avoid the glare of the
many. Still, those who've already begun their morning fitness
ritual, glance in my direction.

I am nineteen stones, four pounds and the shape of the
number eight. It's a big eight, an eighty, a one hundred and

eight. My navy swimming costume is drawn tight over me, like calfskin over a drum. Stares from the early birds are disapproving. They crawl the length of the water and lift their judging eyes up to me when they surface for air. I know the message on each of their faces.

They think I'm indulgent, a bun eater, a lover of sliced bread and thick butter. They think I'm lazy and lie like a big marshmallow on my bed. They think I'm dead inside and eat to find emotional warmth. Populist theories are never wasted on the population.

I want to wipe the expressions from their faces. My voice trembles in my throat, preparing for an outburst. I want to ask them if their opinions could be wrong. I'd like to put it to them that fat people might be the only true hedonists, that eating is a manifestation of the most profound urge to live. I'd like them to search through their modern knowledge to see if thinness is a sign of spiritual deprivation. The attendant prevents my oratory.

'Can you swim, love?'

Yes I can swim. My hesitation vanishes as I walk to the deep end and climb into the water. Like any other body, mine floats. In water we are equal. I swim, awesome as a liner through a sea of pitying sailboats. Feeling as though I have something to prove, I swim ten lengths without stopping and leave myself breathless. For the next half-hour I have to take things easy.

Schoolchildren arrive for lessons at nine o'clock so I give myself plenty of time to leave the water and change. From the spectators' gallery I watch as the last of the early birds finish their swim and a pack of bony children form a line along the edge of the water. In their costumes I can see the ones who will turn to fat if they're not careful with food. Each one of them has skill. Some move quickly through the water, or perform gymnastics. Others dive. It's the diving that makes me sit forward in my chair. I look for technique amongst the spindly limbs. The attendant fills the vending machine in the spectators' gallery. Cups of dried drinks are stacked inside each other, waiting to fit into place in the machine.

'Kids,' she says to me and rolls her eyes. She follows my gaze to the diving board.

The next time I visit the baths, the early birds are not as interested in me. They give me a cursory glance and add two more lengths to their routine to be on the safe side.

In time I become one of the regulars and almost fit in. A woman asks me my name and her manner lets me know she doesn't think we are equals.

'I think you've lost a few pounds.' The attendant casts a scouring eye over my body. She's right and I smile a modest amount of pleasure. I don't tell her that I've lost a stone. It's hardly missed on a frame like mine.

'I used to be weighty,' she says, 'but I got food poisoning one year, lost a load of weight and it never came back.' Her understanding and sympathy aren't unkind. She shouts out to the early birds that I've lost a few pounds and I'm surprised when they cheer. The attention is embarrassing but from then on I'm given recipes by those early birds who tell me they have to battle with weight. When I'm seventeen and a half stones I treat myself to a new costume. It's purple with a navy trim. The attendant notices. She looks at me for some time as though she's hatching a plan and for the first time I feel uncomfortable with her.

'Shift another half-stone, love and I'll whiz the cover back on the diving pool for you. You can dive, can't you?'

The incentive is potent but the half-stone proves stubborn.

I'm hungry when I go to bed and when I wake up. I try to kick-start my metabolism using techniques I've read about in books. It's a while before the seven pounds go. The attendant notices before I tell her.

'It's written all over your face,' she says. 'I'll sort something out. Come Wednesday, as we open, and it's all on for the dive.'

I'm pleased with my weight loss but don't know where I'll get the incentive to lose more. I can fit into smaller clothes than I used to wear but they're still large and rustle on my body when I move. The dive provides me with excitement and focus. After I've done it I'll make up my mind about what to do next with my weight.

I arrive as early as I can on the Wednesday. The regular early birds are right behind me, determined not to miss the action. We offer titbits of conversation to each other but the dive is the real issue and the tension is palpable. No one looks at me as I take my clothes off and leave the changing rooms but their murmuring is animated and excited. Behind me I hear the slap of women's feet on wet tiles. We pass the men's changing rooms and I hear the heavier thud of their feet as they join us.

'Ready, love?' The attendant raises her eyebrows and nods her question at me. I nod my reply and she starts to pull back the blue curtain which separates the diving pool from the rest of the baths. Acres of plastic sheeting are pushed across a heavy metal pole. They rest in stiff folds at one side and I move forward.

The diving pool is deep and tranquil, the air around it is humid and smells of chlorine. There is hardly enough air for me, let alone the others who have come to watch.

As I climb the steps to the boards, the early birds line the pool and look on. I pass the lower two boards and sense a ripple of tension. They can't wait. At the top, butterflies are unleashed in my stomach and I have to pause for breath. Beneath me, the attendant looks small but her expression is as open as ever. She gives me the thumbs-up and I walk to the edge of the board.

Everyone is nervous, expecting to see me snap the board and tumble down like an elephant. They dread, yet lust after my misfortune. My steps are even and quick. The board flexes, rising and falling as I choose my moment. And then I dive. The board clatters one last time and I'm airborne. I am a jumbo jet of a woman, a flying dolphin. My posture is beautiful, I'm not as rusty as I thought. For a split second I'm suspended like a letter U in the air, then I fall with my arms pointing like divining rods into the blue water. There is no comic book splash of a fat girl hitting water; there are no tidal waves, no drowned onlookers. The water opens up and welcomes me. I am as beautiful as a plum falling into thick cream. For a while I plummet into the depths then rise again, a gargantuan cork in the civic baths.

The dive was virtually perfect. Now I'm ready for my *pièce de résistance*.

I've never drawn attention to myself before and have stuck to breaststroke and the occasional crawl in order to blend in. When I re-emerge from the forgiving water I give my audience the best treat yet. I do butterfly stroke to the edge of the pool and then back again. The water heaves and crashes as I smash it with warrior arms. I am a sight to see. The display of my skills isn't wasted on the early birds and attendant who have formed a silent audience.

Light-headed with exertion I leave the diving pool and stride confidently to the main pool. My thighs tremble and rub together at the top, my body quivers. The early birds and the attendant cheer and whistle.

'Bloody great, that was. Roll off the next half-stone.' The attendant pulls the plastic curtain back into place and everything returns to normal.

For the first time since I've been going to the baths I have a shower. I pick a moment when no one is around and take my costume off. The water is hot and gorgeous. I lather myself with soap that smells of lemons and wash my hair with shampoo from a sachet. When I rinse the soap from my eyes and push water away from them with my fingers, I see the attendant. She has been looking at me and isn't stirred from her observations when I turn to face her. As always, she's calm and all seeing and makes no bones about her wish to see me naked. Her eyes discover me from head to toe. I am a majestic woman and she knows this.

The main course

Today you are Cape Malay,
enticing me with spices,
your rich sauce blending with
the Knysna pot. From your fingers
come fennel, cinnamon and coriander,
an earthy rainbow dipping down
to your dish of burnished gold.

Slowly, throughout the day,
you are simmering for me.

When the sun is pulsing amber
in an evening sky, you will let
this aromatic dew, full of butter-rich
brinjies and capsicums, pour

upon my white rice; it will spread
dark upon my china and seep
into the yeast holes of my torn bread,
your taste lingering on my burning lips
until morning.

Just the usual?

I should have worn make-up
I say this every time. Relentless neon,
I despise the way you show up craggy jowls,
the cross-stitch borders round suspicious eyes.
Wet fringe slicked back, I reflect on my image.
Eyebrows should be plucked.

My instant coffee wears a prickly froth
of split ends breezed over by the zealous sweeper,
her face glowing sixteen with a generous dollop
of Body Shop. My reflection reminds me,
must buy coverup.

Soon I will smile. No,
I am not going out tonight.
Yes, it has turned chilly.
My holidays are not yet planned
and yes, it is just the usual.

A serviceable cut which varnished fingers
will tease with mousse, blow into grey crested waves,
hot tonging a bouffant helmet soon sprayed into submission.
My second smile beams from the mirror.
Lovely. (Twelve pounds and a tip.)
Straight home, taps on full,
finger dry to kinked mop that is me.
Just the usual.

Eight years of weaving...

eight years of weaving two lines together.
We want brocades,
rich tapestry to appear
from these strands:
we wish for gold but
sometimes ply the poorest threads, worn
thin by life. My hope
is that when your thread
is taut and tense,
mine can take the strain,
that the cloth will not be filled
with uneven weaving,
that neither will twine around the other
so that the pattern is lost. Thank you for all the
times when your thread
has been like rope
and borne
my extra burden,
for the days and nights
that it has draped soft like silk,
drawing us together.
Thank you for knowing
that two threads are not
enough, for always seeking
to have that three strand
cord of gold
in all we are
and do
and live.

U *neven* *weaving*

Look at his face now, remember him this way
while he is fully innocent of her schemings.
Do not for a moment think she will relent,
kiss him goodbye, call it a day. He thinks
he chose her in that first flush of love,
but she knew his every movement then
and does today. Like a spider she laid strand
upon strand of sweetness, tempted him to change
direction, knew that he would stay, just as she
knows now that another's eyes have lined him up
as prey. She would have forgiven him a little slip,
a surreptitious sip of something new,
but not the reckless gulping, the quenching of desire,
the public abandonment of values he once knew. Watch
now as they walk in the wind, meeting he thinks to tie
up loose ends, part as friends; such foolish schemes.
Even as he rushes home to dial the notes of love's new song
her busy fingers spin thin harmonies, begin the unravelling.

CATHERINE CONZATO

Cartography

He was a thin painter. He'd grown up fearing there were fissures in his mind, such was the incandescence that rippled through there. A feverish child, he talked of light, chasing its plumes. From a young age his tables were compositions. The steep shadow of an old mug; the territory of a battered fork. He sat down, hands clasped, thumbnail tracing a button, eyes plotting.

He wore grey baggy trousers and shaved his head. His ears were small honeyed buckles too low down, accentuated by the bowl of his cranium. He wore a whistle. He always wore a whistle. His nose was proud and wide and fluttery and he was able to hitch his nostrils as he talked. They creased into the wide berth of his smile. With tools, he could chisel a wall: daub it with mud. He painted signboards with a sable brush his grandfather stole from a minister's wife. He painted tarts in town on canvas, and barbershop boys' slick profiles.

When he arrived in the city he was makeshift, recently

bereaved and possessed by the shape of a splatter of white paint on a village girl's bum. He knew he would make it.

Della and Luce were at each other's throats. Della was swimming in a greasy humid vacuum. She'd brought her Ph.D. in fifteenth-century oriental trading economies to West Africa and found herself arranging bougainvillaea and bird of paradise in vases. Luce derided her lack of simplicity. She swallowed glass and detested the white-planed house. She would sit on a watchman's bony chair under the palm nut tree, watching Stephan gallivant about with a ball, the local kids running circles around him. She rolled joints and flicked their damp stubs into the grass. The gardener glanced around at her, then resumed sweeping meticulous piles of leaves. The sky was empty and clean. At intervals, shaky African DC10s spluttered and pulled up into it. There were vultures, but real ones here.

If Della had never walked into that café in Stuttgart looking for her German-loving friend Stacey Mahler she would never have ended up at the bar with Luce and his odd, leggy son. Luce who was leaving for West Africa in a week; Luce who said *There are other worlds* while exerting a take-it-or-leave-it pressure on her knee. Della wrote to Stacey a month later from the rainy season, half deluded by the stinking multifarious setting, half drenched by Luce's unfiltered sexual coaching. What Della had been told afterward was that Luce's thirty-six-year-old wife Chanel had perished in a plane crash on a runway in northern Nigeria. If Della had siphoned off moments of the tragedy to crystallise her own mortality, she was also conscious of being a fast substitute. Uneasy, beyond her climax of flames and metal she might think: Luce had made love to a woman who had *died*.

But Luce became a man with even less endearing baggage. At the embassy he played second fiddle. He was the one who brought in unfortunate dead Germans from car wrecks and questioned bandaged girlfriends weeping rivulets of tears. He saw the bodies into the mortuary, called parents back home in centrally heated apartments, zipped the black plastic bag before all was loaded into the embassy regulation pine coffin. He dealt with the druggies, girls who'd had their passports nicked by Rastas on the beach, the godforsaken marriages. It was no wonder he was first out of the office, first on the tennis courts, first and last at Ryans or Aquarius or Chesters or any bar-of-the-moment. Della's infatuation did not survive its second blow and a lasting creepiness. But she'd left a good job with a claim that her libido had hit the ceiling. She couldn't go back to colleagues with her tail between her legs. In the shadows, in the air-conditioned bedroom shadows where the electricity had as many hiccups as her desire, she willed herself to touch him.

At the university nobody wanted her. She laid out her credentials to disenchanted faces of the exhausted regime. *Oriental what*? They were hardly interested. *We have no use for that*, they tut-tutted, wearing thinning shirts and dull eyes. She hung out at the French Alliance, where coffee and bean cakes were served and met an agile painter arranging his works. A springy man in relief against the hard walls, whom she watched joist a couple of frames together. The big-bellied French director walked in from the corridor and stood in a corner of the room.

He spoke in nasal Parisian twang; the African replied in cocky patois. Della shifted on the plastic chair. When the fat guy left she walked over.

The first man Efua Sarpong loved was a painter from her village. He didn't like girls much. He had her once, between canvases and tubs of paint. She got a blob of white on her bum that he noticed all of a sudden. The freakiness of its outline on her buttock. He'd made her stand there, naked, which she liked and would still become wet should she think about it. But Henry Boateng went to the city without scraping the paint off. And she never washed it. She was exceedingly careful in the shower never to throw water over it. But all the same it cracked and dwindled. She even wore no underwear beneath her shift so that it might stay longer, and visited Boateng's small house on the Elubo road that he might rediscover her like this. But it never occurred. Her bottom itched. She resisted. Finally there was a tiny white speck on her round bluey buttock no bigger than the tip of a biro. She picked it off and ate it.

Luce organised the national day reception on the ambassador's lawn, calling in a dance troupe with drummers. He imported salami and heavy yellow cheese and frozen pretzels the ambassador's wife kindly revived and presented in baskets. But the wine was South African. That was virtually *de rigueur* now for all but the French. There were nine hundred invitations. Of course only two hundred and fifty would show. Della arrived late in a violently patterned off-the-shoulder thing from which her neck and head emerged as grim survivors. Heavy earrings bounced against her throat. Her cropped hair pleated in sweaty channels. Luce watched Della with the consul's wife, coldly making small talk, gracelessly accepting a glass of plonk. He thought of Chanel, as he often did when his second wife's failures were apparent. Their life flashed before him in a harried whiz, an infusing sensation more than a vision, with the trappings of odour, touch, plunging. For a second he felt a flush that squeezed his gut and flooded him with the articulated illusion of a tremendous reality. His pores filled. He looked around and Della was still there, bent to a rag doll woman with marionette hands.

He could afford to move away. He checked on the savouries; went down to the bottom of the lawn to centre a skewwhiff ground light that was shining in people's eyes. He stood by the dancers. Three young girls were thrusting their spines in and out as though they were whipping sticks. Their bent arms jerked around their torsos. The whites of their cheeky eyes flickered and vanished.

'Quite a spectacle,' an entranced European next to him pointed out over the drums. 'Is that a war dance?'

Luce was a practised conversationalist and a bit of a poser. 'Not at all. It's a courtship dance. They come on quite strong.'

'Is that so?'

Luce sized up the guy. Of the expats there were the rugged singles who'd end up with petite, giggly lovers. Or the wife-at-home types who went for broody heavy-arsed vamps. Then there were the pricks who would bend over backwards pretending they never even laid eyes on their raw curves and market dresses. Luce saw he was wearing a greasy tie and a linen jacket that hadn't been pressed: a rugged single. 'It's a cultural thing.'

'I've heard they're very promiscuous. Would there be a lot of, you know, sickness here, on account of that?'

'Sickness?'

'You know, *sickness*.'

Luce saw how the man shook a little, pressing his difficult point, bubbles of sweat covering the surface of his face, dribbling down his neck on to his wet collar, sticking the shirt to his hairy chest. Luce knew that in a year he would see this man in a bar with a rowdy group of skinny girls and a couple of white stodgy ringleaders with bald heads and damp grey cocks in their trousers. They would pretend never to have met.

'Oh, you mean AIDS. Oh, yes. Rotten way to go. We've lost a few. It comes on so slowly. You hardly know you have it and then – *clunk* – it'll come up on some blood test and you'll remember the girl but she'll be dead in her village, then you'll just start withering . . .' Luce left him staring at the dancers.

He walked up behind Manning Rosier, on the population control programme, bathing in her aura for a second before grasping her forearm and lightly swinging her around. Manning was the first woman he made love to after Chanel's death. She was a husky American who wore two-bit clothes and bad haircuts. She'd understood him. He looked down at her radiance. 'Still screwing away?' he whispered as he kissed her cheek.

'It's better than you've had all month.'

'I don't doubt it.' He laughed.

He moved on, saluting people, occasionally extending his arm and shaking the hand of an ambassador or hotel manager, ably making small talk, sampling the food and gulping the commendable wine. He glimpsed Della and his first impulse was to turn away swiftly. But she had seen him. From the way her eyes caught and widened he knew she had seen him searching for an escape. Helplessly disarmed, he looked at her, hating the change of mood she was already capable of inflicting upon him. The drums garbled from somewhere deep behind the crowd. He thought of a dry bed, a loving woman, being luminously happy.

Kofi was the boy who came to clean their shoes on Sunday mornings when Stephan's father was still in bed. He wore the same brown torn shirt and busted trousers every week. When Stephan gave him a New Yorkers baseball cap he wore that too, although Della said he should never take it back again. When Kofi slowly walked up the steps and knocked on the glass where Stephan was watching television, Stephan would turn off Cartoon Network and begin to collect the family's shoes. He took one of Della's stripy baskets and looked under all the living-room chairs. He crept upstairs into their bedroom where they lay with a big gap down the middle of the sheets. He piled in Della's high-heeled leather sandals (she was short) and the sweaty loafers she wore in the day. He took out his father's enormous shoes with their thin laces and pushed them all in. He went into his own room and grabbed his old, too-small Birkenstocks that he loved because his mum used to buckle them up. He grabbed his school sandals – they were cheap old things Della had brought back from the second-hand market saying that they were as good as new but they weren't.

The basket was heavy. He pushed their bedroom door closed and laboured down the stairs. Then he put it down on the parquet floor and slid it the rest of the way with his foot. When Kofi saw him he would pull himself up and stand at the glass door but Della said he should never come inside. Kofi picked up the basket in the doorway. He looked strong for a thin kid.

Stephan helped him lay out all the shoes in big pairs and little pairs; high pairs and fat pairs; black pairs and dark red pairs. It was cool on the veranda. Kofi took out his three tins of nugget – black, brown and neutral – and the dirty rag he spat on first. Stephan climbed up on to the big cane chair and sat back to watch.

Each pair of shoes Kofi scrubbed with nugget and then shined with a second dirty rag. 'The brown ones aren't shiny enough,' Stephan might say from his chair. Or, 'You should get that bit of dirt off the bottom of the heel there.' Kofi did everything. Stephan knew how much he should pay him. Afterwards they went down on to the grass and kicked a ball until it was too hot.

'Who's that?' Della pointed, aware that there would be another secretive and beguiling story attached to the image.

'Oh, a woman.'

'I can see that, Henry.'

'A woman from my village.'

'Why does she have that white patch on her bum? Did you sleep with her?'

'I don't remember. I don't remember anyone before you.'

'That's cute.'

'Will you undress?'

'You're not painting me.'

She crawled towards him, her face creased and her eyes smaller and shinier. He stepped forward although she stopped before the end of the divan, sitting back on her mauve haunches. He licked her face, she put her large hands on his thighs. They kissed.

He lay down by her, awaiting her hands on his belt and zipper. She stalked him there, pulling open cloth, exhibiting his flesh she stroked calmly.

He lifted her skirt and felt around her bottom, smoothing his palm on her downy flesh. They were lovers, he thought greedily, watching her profile at work on him, her mouth sucking and cooing and claiming him. He thought of her husband, now on mission in some ramshackle village bowing to a semi-illiterate, bamboozled chief. Throwing his head backward in delight, he saw one of his paintings from a new, astonishing angle. He thought, I *will work on that as soon as she is gone.*

His own excitement propelled him toward her, almost pushing her off to pin her to the sheets. He was hard and big from being played with. She too surged at him, wrinkling under his torso to get her pelvis on to him. She shot down, taking him in gorgeous surprise as she sealed his lips.

Luce looked at the thousand and one fillings in Manning Rosier's teeth as she laughed her Yankee laugh again. 'I didn't know your teeth were so bad. I'd never have kissed you so much,' he complained.

'Oh Luce!' She scratched her scalp, fiddled with an azure blue bead necklace (the only pleasing article he'd ever seen her wear) and avoided eye contact. Manning had said she cared. That is why they were here at the Canadian café, discussing what Della must have been doing in Luce's jeep on the Winneba road, with a shirtless Henry Boateng lolling out of the window. Or why Della caught sluggish taxis across town to Henry's studio and came home just before the school bell with a rubbed face and screaming knees. 'Don't you think she deserves it?' Manning was testing him. 'We've all had our beat around the bush.'

'How can I say? I'm the last one to speak of Della's obligations. I just provide life experience for gullible Westerners.'

'Why be bitter? You've known the girl for all of six months.'

'You can screw up a lot in six months.'

'So I've seen. Let her go, why don't you?'

Luce let his hand wander toward her forearm. He stroked it; the movement had been a prelude of theirs.

'Uh-uhh,' she drew away. 'I've got a full house.'

'Is he that good? I'm envious.'

'No you're not, you're just on dry ground. Sort it out, Luce.'

He decided to confront Della when Stephan had gone to bed. Della tucked herself into the divan with a novel. She had prepared lemongrass tea for them both. Luce read an English newspaper. He glanced at her as he sipped his tea. Her face looked older and thinner than the edgy pale girl who had stepped into the café in Stuttgart. This was the woman he had courted with more fervour than ever in his life. Her capitulation had been the most generous reward. She looked placid; she read keenly. Her sleeveless shirt revealed arms that were firmly shaped. Unable to find a decent job, she had taken to the gymnasium for the first time in her life. Luce waited for a signal from his feelings. Who was he to disturb the forces at work?

Efua Sarpong went to the city and saw Henry Boateng's name on a big banner across a main street. The next morning she went to the painting exhibition at the hotel. She walked around the empty lobby looking at the canvases. She saw Henry sitting at a desk flicking through an *obroni* magazine. Since she had been in the city she had eaten *kenke* and smoked fish day and night and dreamed of sleeping in Henry Boateng's arms. She walked over to him in her hot stretchy yellow dress. 'Did you love me?'

'Efua?'

'Did you love me?'

'When?'

'The first time. It was hot, it was stifling. You said—'

'I don't remember what I said. It is useless to speak in those moments.'

'I don't believe so.'

At noon Efua Sarpong took off her yellow dress and made love to Henry Boateng for the second time in her life. She left on her headscarf. He wore a whistle on a dirty braided cord. He rolled her five times down the bed and made her come to a stop on her back. He walked around above her head. She heard the whistle beat against his chest and his heels on the linoleum of his room. She stretched out her full length so that her feet and hands dropped over either edge of the mattress. Wet again, she closed her eyes and heard nothing. Or perhaps liquid, something spilling. She thought of her mother, remembering the knobs of her spine as she undressed. She sat up, looking around for her lover. Henry Boateng came at her with a dripping purple brush and began with her breasts.

Bats shook into the sky. Many still hung along the , kitsch leather handbags squawking. The air was putrid with their droppings, shrill with their sonic gabble. She had lost her way again. They were still parallel to the main road, whose afternoon traffic she could hear shunting towards Sankara Circle beyond the buildings. Stephan held his plaster cast with his free hand and shook it. He pulled a ten-centimetre rule from his pocket and poked between the cast and his yellowed skin. He scratched. 'I'm hot, Della. I'm hot, I said.'

The grey wood-planked wards had extended much further

than she'd imagined, each gloomy barrack with its crooked and missing opaque louvres joined to the next by an asbestos-canopied walkway.

Occasionally, patients passed them. Wicked old women from the bush who refused to die. Old men with milky eyes full of storms. Della asked a nurse in a green tunic the way to the orthopaedic surgeon. They were told to round the next ward, cross a courtyard and ask. They walked out under the sky as bats deserted a nearby tree with screeching vehemence. Della and Stephan watched the angry creatures schlock this way and that, some entangling with each other, some scooting off on wild tangents. Then they registered the shots. Some of the unhappy beasts thunked to the ground. The rest jerked this way and that, a group of schoolgirls shrieking off into skeins of doom.

Stephan halted above one of the animals. He crouched. Della stood next to him. The bat rolled over, clawing the earth with the webbed hands attached to its cloak. A whiny sound came from its grimacing mouth. 'There's no wound,' Stephan said. 'It looks like it just fell.'

Della's stare moved from the bat to the back of Stephan's head. His hair was very white and coarse like the synthetic hair of a doll. She realised she had never touched the two cords at the back of his neck and felt a peculiar warm desire she supposed might echo the pull of motherhood. Quite prominently, nobody ever spoke of Luce's lost wife.

'It can't stand up to fly again. The legs aren't strong enough,' he said. He turned around and looked at her. 'It'll die, you know. Just because it fell out of the tree.'

The animal writhed, tearing at the cloth of its own belly. Della looked away at the bleached sky with its filter of harmattan cloud. The sun's heat produced a pressure behind this that seeped into her brain. Her skin was liquid. She thought of her head on Henry Boateng's belly. His scent of canvas and thinners.

But then she remembered what she had seen in Boateng's studio the last time. The canvas he wouldn't show her. It was a huge tapering tree with python-like branches wrestling the sun. High up, her effort and nakedness exposed, there was a white woman climbing. The brush strokes were loose and unkind, making her into a kind of feral monster. Della had driven home crazily in the jeep, crying.

That night, before Luce bent over her with great draughts of hope, she rang Boateng's number and told him the affair was over.

Della and Stephan reached a broken veranda whose cast cement foundations stood naked in the dirt. The door was open. An army doctor bent over a screaming child with its legs tossed crudely on the bed. There was a bench outside. On it, a row of faces seemed ever so silent.

For a boy whose parents were anxious about travel

First, a boy will appear.
It will have been raining
and he will be familiar with fog and wet.
He will know every moth from where he lives
as far as Brazil, their creamy fur
their urgent need for light
how they launch from the diamond tips
of grasses into the milky night.

After years as a government clerk in a small town
he will find himself at a frontier
without passport or wallet.

He will find he has already learned
to survive and will leave his maps
under the waterfall.

On a night with no promise of morning
he will wake to the muffled voices of moths
he will find himself walking towards
what will have grown inside him.

He will find he can be the taste of grass
can be aimless flight, a resting on peeling bark
pressing his folded wings deeper under the calyx
his skin veined with unreadable directions.

Coming clean

I kissed him for the first and only time, and walked up
the ravine at Novo Horizonte without once looking back.
He had a nose for history, a sulphur-crested cockatoo,
he was as fresh as the rainforest. That was seven years ago.

I'm still pursuing my question
I hurled at him as he told me to catch up with him in another
century.
Sometimes a hot wind teases me with the perfumes
of 100-year-old roses and mission bibles.

I live with the woman who makes me happy in Uruguay,
we collect angel fish and cast runes on the beach.
She knows my question is grinding me smooth
as moon-washed pebbles. She has the blessed
determination of an otter, she prises me open
gently as a sea urchin. My irises have faded to horizon blue.
I'm coming clean as sucked coral. He will not recognise me.

Prague, November 1999

You will think it is spring
when this letter arrives
even though you will always have been waiting
for the iced pear tree buds
the yellow light melting the snow
on the broken benches in the park
you will say you have wasted years
wanting what I never gave.

You expected me to live without my passport.
I thought it was love but you were so busy
proving there is only one language.
All I want is a new way of saying things.

Don't answer me back.
Meine liebe Freundin, erinnere Dich an mich.

I wanted you and then I let you go
I don't want to come back
but I want you to be happy
when you get to the embassy
you can use what I wrote
and the photo I took
of the way you looked
when I believed every word you said.
I want you to remember me like this.

The hottest night for 47 years

The heatwave was 47 years coming,
since your birth the summer nights have been chill;
now you're sweating and they've got you naked
in the house and won't let you take your clothes.

Sitting in a row of girls in a beechwood aisle
learning about rubber trees, you smooth your dress
over your knees, gazing outward beyond the plantation,
beyond paying attention, past years of geography

into the place where birds go when they die,
dropping through the branches on to the floor
piled up with the litter of generations, and
filling the world with unstoppable light.

BARBARA MARSHALL

A n n i v e r s a r y

Each year my husband fashions me a gift; our anniversary is always marked by the present. He was the first dark man I saw on New Year's morning and we were wed on Valentine's Day. For the first anniversary, our cotton wedding, he made me a pincushion of red cotton velvet in the shape of a heart, stuffed with cotton rags. He was not skilled with the needle and the stitches were puckered and uneven around the edge; but I could feel how much loving work he had put into its making by the tiny scabs on his palms and raw tips of his fingers. The pincushion rested plump and plush on the shiny black board of the Singer machine as I sat sewing tiny shirts in preparation for our baby.

On our paper wedding, he gave me a papier mâché egg he had built up tissue by tissue; its finish was perfectly smooth and lacquered a deep crimson. Our initials were inlaid in mother of pearl, opalescent letters entwined. He had spent many nights in his attic room between Christmas and

Valentine's Day while I waited downstairs, cradling the baby or rocking myself back and forth on the carved iron treadle. His eyes were deeply shadowed and crimson drops had crusted under his fingernails. On Sundays, we wrapped the baby in his lacy shawl and walked together in the park: it did us both good to get out of the house and take the air. We always took the same paths, strolling past the Villas set back behind the elm trees which were budding with spring. We dreamed of moving into the Villas. We curled up together at night on the sofa, talking and weaving plans for the future: the views we would have across the park, the picnics we would take under our trees.

The next year was the coldest January of my life, without my husband beside me, only the baby asleep in his cot. Each night I went to sleep alone as he worked above me in his room. I knew when he crept into our bed because he brought the sharp smell of disinfectant with him; it had permeated his skin and when I turned to kiss the small hairs on his neck, they tasted of brine. Of course, I never opened his letters or any of the many-shaped deliveries that arrived with every New Year. That year there had been a parcel from America which was marked HEMLOCK BARK; I couldn't help but read it. In fact he asked me straight away if I had taken notice of the label. I think that was the first time I lied to him, although really, I cannot be sure of that. On our third anniversary, our leather wedding, he gave me a cushion of the softest, palest kidskin. It had a nap like satin velvet, the bloom and silkiness of our baby's cheeks. Although the salty tang of curing lingered for weeks on the stairs, my husband was beside me again at last, stroking the down on my thighs and the milky moon of my pregnant belly. He loved me so much. When I passed down the drive by the Villas I had the feeling he was there with me, even though by then I often walked by myself.

There were many days when we could not go out and then my small son would climb on the armchair and open the big cupboard by the fireplace where I kept my porcelain, the forget-me-not bread and butter plates and my bone-handled knives. He would lift these out one by one and arrange them in a circle in front of the fire while I nursed the baby. He specially liked to take down the miniature teapot with the broken lid which was kept on the mantelpiece for his games. It was turquoise bone china and decorated with a pink shepherdess cameo which my son turned carefully to face him. He would play like this for hours. I did not like to stay in so much and I would take any little bit of sun in the yard, making cuttings from geraniums and potting them up on the old washstand by the back door. I loved the strong smell of their stems that cracked with juice and the furriness of their leaves. It was the flower and fruit anniversary that year and my husband gave me a polished apple and a bowlful of stiffened silk tulips. The tulip in the centre had its petals spread to show little black wire tongues; the others were all closed, swollen and scarlet. We always went out on our wedding anniversary and as we pushed the pram through the front door, I found a single red rose on the step, dewy and crisp, and I turned to my husband. He was not smiling.

Although he threw away the rose after the questioning was over, I slipped out that night and found it. I did not dare keep it of course, but I breathed in its scent and rubbed the petals between my fingers before hiding it in the holly hedge. Even though Valentine's Day had passed, my husband often stayed in the attic room now, coming to bed in the middle of the night, his breathing rough and troubled. That winter when I was making the curtains, I found that my dressmaking pins were all rusting. They could be scraped out, stiffly, from the pincushion; but although their heads were shiny, the pins were brown. I could not use them because they left red prick marks in the cloth. I asked my husband if I could buy some more. When I returned with my purchase, he observed that I had been away a long time getting pins and I said that I had stayed in the park with the children playing. I told him that I hadn't seen anyone and I had walked home by the elm driveway. I turned away from him and I pinched each of the old pins out of the cushion. The last one dripped rusty red drops on my hand. I did not want to put my bright new pins in there, but my husband was watching me. His smell was very sweet and his hands were dusty with sugar, but the air on the stairs was horribly sickly and it thickened downstairs in our room. I had a gluey feeling in the back of my throat and the baby coughed and cried as I pushed in the pins, one by one.

His present to me that year was a handmade box full of sugar candy and jewel-coloured Turkish delight. I could hardly bear to swallow them but he watched me pick out and eat the frosted sapphire jellies and then he went to the front door. When he returned, he carried back a chocolate heart. I could not explain it to him and then he plunged his fist into my bowl of silk tulips. They sighed as the air rushed out from them in a puff of sour, sulphurous mist; and their black tongues cracked. When I went out of the house, I would make the children ready secretly and have the pram poised by the front door and then I would fly off down past the elm trees, knowing he was somewhere behind them. On the way back, I would note, from the rustle and shadow, which of the trees hid him, and I would know how much time I had. It was never long enough to get into the attic room.

I have cried many tears into the kidskin cushion. My wet cheeks spotted the chamois and in places it started to crust with salty white stains and I noticed how its pungency was increasing until I could not bear its rich leathery stink any-where near me. I do not know why it was so fetid, or why the mould grew green over the mother-of-pearl inlay on my papier mâché egg. Every night now, he was taken up with working on my new present and dust was flowing down the stairs, silting up on every step and sifting downwards. Every morning he fol-lowed me to the elm trees and when I came in he asked me where I had been. I told him I had only taken our son to school but sometimes, when I hurried along the drive, I caught a glimpse of myself darting off through the trees. My husband asks because he loves me but he cannot trust me. When he hears the tapping of my brush and pan on the stairs, I know he freezes in the attic room, I can sense how his breath is held as he lurks and there is a bristling in the air, like I feel in the park when I am waiting.

The box my husband carved for me on our wooden wedding will not open, even though I have tried to prise it with a knife. Of course he noticed the scratches on its beautifully polished grain and I could not think of an answer. He stroked the box with one hand and my face with the other and his hands were yellow waxed and smelt so richly resined that I felt my cheek turning sallow under his touch, my throat blocked. He asked me if I had received any other gifts and I told him no. I hid the tiny carved ivory hare, which I had found on the front wall, at the bottom of a geranium cutting where my fingers can push through the soft compost to find it, each time upsetting the new bleached roots. I move the pots around on the washstand, so the plant that fails to thrive is not so obvious. I can tell its stalk, however, withering and browning, and I worm in my hand to its cool smoothness.

My husband's hands are splayed like a waxwork's, the joints are gnarled with all his work, the palms are leathered. When I step outside the door, I feel myself lift into the air, disappear in the trees. Sometimes, when I pick up my son from school, some person will stop me to talk. Sometimes, I do not know where the time goes. When it pours with rain, I stand at the gate and feel the hem of my coat to see if it is wet enough, before I enter the house. My son and the baby stare at their father when he meets us at the front door. Sometimes he stands at the Singer and stabs each pin to the head in the pincushion, while behind him my son piles up the plates, with their chipped edges eating into the forget-me-nots, and then my son rattles the knives, loosening the blades from the bone.

The sawdust ripples into sand dunes at the bottom of the attic staircase. Each night his foot makes a print; each morning it has drifted over. My own footprints disappear the same way, as soon as they are made: I know he examines the sand, like he examines my body. He licks the fair hairs around my navel so they stick backwards; he traces for fingerprints with his finely dusted thumb.

The pincushion sits in a sticky russet pool on the Singer. The machine's leather strap hangs loose now, disconnected by my husband after the needle lowered through my finger, locking it to the plate. My husband said it was my pronubial finger, the one with the nerve connected to the heart, the wedding finger.

KATHERINE FROST

F o r t u n a t e   e p i s o d e s

After the unfortunate episode in the Garden of Eden . . . most thought of snakes is of envenoming . . .
(Serpentes, of the order of Squamata, Encyclopaedia
Britannica, 15th edn, 1974–94, vol. 26)

In the dim hall where they're housed
                    she sets before us her tribe Serpentes:
                              which began

as lizard, but got down
                    into the rind of the planet
                              where the gaps are, let go

arms, legs, voice, eyelids, a lung –
                    learned to live
                              with what's on offer.

She numbers its poisons:
the kind that makes you
bleed from every hole –

you die bruised black all over;
the kind that scrambles what the nerves
tell each other,

the powerlines cancel like a war –
you're crushed out of
breath by your ribs;

the kind that goes straight to your heart
and stops it.

And when
the last of us has filed out,
her creatures are safe under glass,
when she's checked

the heat and the oily drinking pools
and let in the silly, scrambling mice
whose shrieks

the snakes can't hear – when she's home,
she'll tell her man
about the coupling;

about how – it may be just after
the hibernation sleep that
could have become its last,

or it may be just before each by itself slips down
        to a dark it can't choose
               to wake from –

the male finds the female
        by the taste of the earth where she's been,
            which he sips

with his liquorice twist of
        tongue, spooling in and up
            to the alert

hidden place on his palate
        that came into being to know this,
            the slick of pheromones;

about how, when he has found her
        he laps his body along her body,
            nailhead

to fluent tip and moulds it to hers;
        and maybe he takes her neck
            in his mouth

as the cobra does – and rears kelim feints
        to sway with her own; or maybe
            he steadies her

with abortive hind limbs, a rump of pelvic girdle,
        as the python does;
            either way –

her throat, her underbelly bared, reaching
for his unarmed caress –
he clasps her also

from the inside with a
hemipenis – its spinules,
flounces, calyces.

There can be, our snakekeeper
will remind her man, neither shy
nor ecstatic

closing of eyes –
only a glance, as past a mirror,
and an echo through each

lidless, voiceless escaped lizard:
something not yet
pared from the genome,

that's made it this far,
easing from cool cells
a windfall grace.

S *hark*

From mussel-spiked rocks jutting out
              into where the waves never stop,
one of the fishermen has caught something.
              To the crowd on the shore
a shrimp would be a prize. Leaving our tidepools
              we edge around for a sight of
six foot plus of heavy shouldered sun burnished
              man wrestling with two foot
of enraged thrashing muscle his broad hands
              can just barely keep holding.

A torpedo's dedicated lines you'd think –
              if a torpedo could have the nifty
thalidomide elbow, could hug out to its skin
              with the softsheened exactness
no longer favoured by the seriously rich,
              could unzip a blunt snout – all that
fuselage-silver unpuckered upholstery –
              on a fence of teeth. Sharks
don't rank here with Lord Zedd and Scar: every
              swimming beach has nets
inspected often. There's a stillness
              as the PG movie shot flickers from
head to head: those jaws, those teeth closing
              on a thigh, a little naked midriff.

But our man has the creature clamped
            between seabooted calves; only
the snout and V of a tail can twist
            and rear, we feel the bracing. And we
catch the stare, the pupils two black holes
            that can't close even against this.

Out of nowhere it seems, a knife. Not a
            big one, its focuses the technicians
among us. A boy of about nine wonders
            'What's he going to do?' No answer.
Two heavy palms, one with the knife, are
            working at the mouth, grappling
shoving, but fighting clear of the mangling bite.
            And at last one hand
has got the jaws immobile, agape, thumb and
            forefinger are jammed in
each side below the cheek, deep where a
            shark's jaw will unhinge
top from bottom to widen for the kill. The hand
            with the knife is going down
inside past the teeth. Slacken now,
            they'll have half the forearm.

I'm not sure any more, is this the moment
            when a five-year-old takes his
father's hand, to whisper – the godawful
            tearjerking comic timing of this –
'It's a baby.' When the nine-year-old's
            fingers slip to his own throat where the

Adam's apple is starting. When suddenly
                            it's as if the sea air were no longer
our element, as if that hand with the knife
                            were going down, down inside all our
throats and we have to gag and gag until we can make
                            the whole pitiful business stop.

But even as we think we can't bear it
                            a moment longer, the hand comes up –
with the hook: shows it, high. A gobbet
                            of fat grey fish flesh spiked on to it.
Again, 'What'll he do?'

                            What the fisherman eventually does is let go
the taut stoop of his back. Slowly
                            he straightens, slowly he lifts up
the exhausted thing, holding it, from below
                            the shoulders, very tight
but – do we imagine – tender too, much as
                            you might a baby or small child
that had just almost – thankfully not quite –
                            wrestled free and still could –
it seems to us that really it is
                            not that much bigger than a human baby –
then he turns and strides, fast, up the
                            staired rocks to the top and with a
wide sweep of both arms he slings it –
                            out to where the waves lash up to take it.

I see five years open his mouth to ask, with that
                    terrible directness small children
do eventually learn to protect their
                    parents from: 'Is it going to die?'
He never does ask, because nine years
                    cuts in, man to man, careful:
'Will it be able to swim now?' The fisherman's
                    got his rod back in his hand,
he's glancing round for the greasy tin
                    with the bait, but he looks down
at that to first one saltsticky blond head,
                    then the other. There's – not properly
a pause exactly, the slightest lift of his
                    chin, he might be drawing himself back
from one of those places you don't tell about.
                    And 'Yes' he says, 'Oh yes.'

PENNY SIMPSON

Kissing calico

'The trick is to begin with a solution, then work backwards.'

This was the advice Crawley Hughes gave to Maisie Thomas when he began to teach her mathematics in his kitchen in Cathedral Road. She didn't know of very many solutions, however, and so had to improvise from memory.

'You mean, like: love and marriage equals a horse and carriage, sir?'

Crawley Hughes had laughed, but they persevered. Maisie thought she would never get the hang of sums, but her employer made them seem nothing more threatening than the ordered steps of a favourite dance. Each had its place in the scheme of things. The next step was to learn to tell the time. Crawley Hughes could make the seasons change by turning the hands on his gilt pocket watch. Maisie watched his fingers turn time on its head.

'Out with the old, in with the new, girlie.'

The pocket watch rode next to her employer's pinstriped

trouser leg. He had once let her hold it, so Maisie could see for herself how its hands were turned. It was a beautiful watch, shiny as the knives she had to polish every day. Its gold case was as hot as her breath, because it had been resting against his leg. She returned the watch to Crawley Hughes. His waiting hands were like shovels. The hair from his arm coursed down to the tips of his fingers. Maisie wanted to stroke them, like she did the fur on a cat. He pulled a chair up close to her in the kitchen as she recited her times tables and she sensed the heat he gave off, fiercer than the fire in the grate by her toes. Crawley Hughes always wore his sleeves rolled up, even in the coldest of weathers.

It had been cold when Maisie had arrived at the house in Cathedral Road anxious to find out about a situation advertised in the *Evening Echo* for a 'maid of all work'.

'Will *there be food, Mam?*'

'Will *you let off whining, Maisie. You have to be grown-up now.*'

'But *will there be food?*'

Maisie had been terrified of getting lost in the big three-storey house with nothing to eat. One day, Crawley Hughes had seen her lift an apple from the fruit bowl in the dining room. He had winked and pointed upstairs. Up above their heads, his wife Myrtle lay coughing.

'Nothing said, and you get fed, girlie.'

Maisie had blushed. Later, she had thrown the apple away into the boating lake in the little park she visited on her rare days off. It was not that she felt bad about stealing the apple. She had not liked the air of complicity that had grown up between her and Crawley Hughes. After the apple incident, he seemed always to show up wherever she was working, even in the remotest of corners. Maisie came to feel that he was watching over her.

'I'm not a thief, sir. Please. I won't do it no more.'

'You will not do what any more, girlie?'

'Take food.'

'You're hungry?'

'Yes.'

'Then take what you need. After all, Mrs Hughes rarely eats these days. Take her share.'

Maisie eventually learned to tell the time by watching the hands move on Crawley Hughes' pocket watch, but there were other ways of keeping time. In winter, she stripped green apple wood with her bare hands and fed the sticks into the big kitchen range, while in spring she washed the window nets free from the soot of smoking fires. In summer, Maisie cleaned the cutlery outside, because she could see then just how good she was when she spun her blades up into the glaring sunlight. When winter next came round, Maisie would warm herself up by plunging her bare arms into the washing coppers. Any sheets left hanging outside for too long had to be doused with boiling water from a kettle. Maisie hopped from foot to foot in the snow and sang little bits of song that she had learned at school while she unfroze the bed sheets.

She liked the summer months best of all. Once summer had officially arrived – and it was only official after Crawley Hughes reset his watch – Maisie could abandon her hat. She could walk down to the corner bakery without her thin serge coat on. She could see the blossoms out on the trees in front of the old synagogue and she could catch the sound of birds in the nearby park, which had a boating lake, a hothouse and hundreds of flowers. Each bed of flowers came with a little name tag, written in a funny language which she tried hard to decipher as she dug her bare toes into the park grass.

Myrtle Hughes had once owned a draper's shop nearby. The baker revealed this to Maisie one day. Three months after coming back from honeymoon, Mrs Hughes had retired to her bed and, as far as he could tell, had not emerged from under her quilt since. Her husband did everything for her and Maisie knew that part of his tale to be true. She had been ordered never to enter Myrtle's bedroom. She did occasionally walk into Crawley Hughes's room on the opposite side of the landing to place a stone water bottle at the foot of his bed. It was the size of a box room. The walls were brown, the floor uncarpeted, and the bed as narrow as her own upstairs in the attic. Maisie found this arrangement intriguing.

Her parents slept in a giant-sized bed, which took up nearly the entire floor of their bedroom in the family home in Zinc Street. It was a perilously big place for young children to get themselves lost in, all mysterious curves and dips and the odd loose spring.

When she was little, Maisie and her five older sisters had spent a lot of time ferreting their way into their parents' bed. It was their favourite adventure. Maisie had always slept best curled up between her parents. She had finally been weaned from this habit when she turned nine.

'It's not the done thing any more, Maisie, lovey. Out you go now.'

Her mother had shooed her out of the bed and from that day onwards she had felt like an over-curious pigeon, pathetically hopping around for scraps of affection. Lying in exile on really cold winter nights, Maisie had to breathe over her own sheets in an attempt to warm them. But it was only an echo of the heat that had emanated from her parents' bed. Since leaving them, Maisie had always felt the cold. Only the hottest of suns persuaded her to roll up her sleeves and abandon her hat. Maisie was tiny. Her mam said she had no flesh on her to keep in the heat.

'*Pocket size, pocket wise,*' her father would joke.

This comment puzzled Maisie. What more did she need to know about the contents of pockets? Pockets were places where you kept loose change, handkerchiefs, ticket stubs and sweets. But they could also be places of deep mystery, her father had suggested.

When Crawley Hughes first set his watch before her and she had seen how it captured time with its tiny gold hands, she had wondered if this might not be the mystery her father had been alluding to.

'Is Mrs Hughes really ill, sir? Is she at death's door?'

Crawley Hughes had laughed at her question.

'If she is, he's in need of a bloody loud door knocker! Excuse me, Maisie, but Mrs Hughes has been something of *a trial* during our married life. Her illnesses are, well . . . not real ones. There are difficulties in the way she sees things, compared to, say, how we see things.'

'Can she do the maths right?'

'She can calculate, certainly, Maisie.'

Mr Hughes put his hands together behind his head and leaned back in his chair.

Summer was a-comin' in . . . Summer. Maisie left off wearing her hat and she rolled down her stockings. The sun was beginning to burn through her skin and into her bones. She found herself skipping and running when she visited the park. Winter was gone. Winter. You watched winter unfold in the light given out by candles and fire flames. Summer was light in itself. Maisie polished the chairs in the front room until they shone like the sun outside. She could see the chair legs reflected in the parquet floor. Her hands bled from her efforts. She wrapped them up in loose pieces of calico, the ones not going to be used to boil puddings on a Sunday, and hugged them to her as she sat out in her evenings in the kitchen.

Mr Hughes saw her bandaged hands one night. He said, had there been an accident? And Maisie had said, no, it was the cleaning that did it. You need a servant, girlie, he had replied. They had both laughed. Mr Hughes was in his shirt-sleeves as usual, pushing out heat like a small furnace. Maisie began crying. She had no idea why, but it was something to do with his body heat and his kindness, all mixing in together with her unspent tears. Maisie hadn't really had a good cry since she was kicked out of her parents' bed.

'The sheets, they was so cold. And I was on my own, sir . . . and gawd, what am I saying? Sorry, sir.'

Mr Hughes reached into his pocket and pulled out a handkerchief, which he handed over to Maisie.

'I didn't think you were unhappy, Maisie. I hear you singing out here. And once, in the park, you know, I saw you skip across the grass. Not a care in the world, I thought.'

Maisie tried hard to think of what her particular cares might be, but try as she might she could not put her finger on any one reason for her tears.

'It's like that sometimes, isn't it, sir? It all seems as black as the grate down there. You don't know what will happen next.'

'Yes, that's very true, Maisie. Now, you must give me your word that when you next feel like the inside of that grate, you will tell me? I don't like to think of you crying down here, all alone.'

He turned away from her. Maisie wondered if he often thought of her. She found the idea strange and exciting all at once.

She assumed nobody really thought about her very much, not even her own family. They were so busy squabbling and shouting and laughing and drinking.

'Get off the sidings, and step on the main track.'

'Stop joking me, Da. Please.'

Maisie's father was a signalman on the railways. He made trains stop and start; pulling levers and pressing switches, he made things happen all the time. Maisie was not like that, she never had been, she had always stood firmly on the sidings in spite of her father's exhortations to move on. The main track meant being fast enough to keep up and Maisie had never been one for keeping up. She thought about her abysmal attempts to learn her times tables at school.

Mr Hughes had moved towards the kitchen door. He turned back before he left and smiled at her. Maisie smiled back.

Autumn came and went in a flurry of wet leaves and chilblained fingertips. Maisie shivered when she stepped into the house from the cold streets outside. Mr Hughes lent her his sheepskin gloves one day. They were huge, but her fingers burnt like toast in their grasp. The leather gloves had moulded themselves to fit round Mr Hughes' hands. She could sense them wrapped round her own fingers when she slipped her hands inside her pockets. Deep down in her pockets. *Pocket size, pocket wise.* She was wise about very little, but she felt she was slowly learning something very important. From that day onwards, Mr Hughes always lent her his gloves. She tried returning them when she got back from her walk in the park, but he would put them back inside her pockets and pat her sides, and then, one day, his hands had stayed still on her hips. The furry hands with their square-topped fingers. Maisie had shivered, but she had not been cold. Mr Hughes was only a few inches taller than her and she found herself on a level with his chin. Looking up, she could see into his eyes. His hands were warm on her hips. She placed her own hands on top of his.

'See, sir. They is as warm as yours is now.'

'My name, Maisie, is Crawley. Will you call me Crawley?'

'Yes, sir. Crawley.'

'Knighted by a lady. How fitting.'

He had kissed her forehead and withdrawn his hands. Maisie felt disappointed. She had wanted him to go on holding her. She kept her hands on her hips as she retreated into the kitchen. She was slow, but she was not stupid. Her sisters had told her in soft whispers what they did up on the old race-course with the men they picked up at the cafés in Broadway. Somehow, she couldn't imagine Crawley Hughes lying down on a racecourse. Maisie giggled and then she laughed out loud. No. 'Goings-on' happened best in beds like the one in Zinc Street, with its hot sheets and its loose springs. Maisie had always felt safe in that bed. She wondered if Mr Hughes – if Crawley – would expect her to lie down with him on his bed in the box room. Did she want to lie down with him? She rather thought she did. She jumped up and rescued his gloves from her coat pockets. Slowly, she drew them over her fingers, smoothing over their cracks, thinking all the while of Crawley Hughes's hairy-tipped fingers resting on her hips.

She removed the gloves and hoisted her dress up, laying her fingers against her hip bone to check again the sensation of skin on skin. What did she feel? Just the warm touch of her fingers. Nothing else. She didn't feel the same sensations she had experienced when Crawley had let his hands rest on her body. Then she slowly stroked her hips. Her skin was calico-pale. Her stomach was soft and slightly rounded. She had to pull her dress and slip up even further in order to stroke her stomach. Maisie pushed the palms of her hands down against her stomach and looked up, to find Mr Hughes standing in the kitchen doorway. Neither of them moved for what seemed like an age. Maisie's hands stayed exactly where they were. She caught her breath. Mr Hughes seemed to turn around, but then he was crossing the floor towards her. Maisie's heart thumped so hard, she thought it might jump out of her chest. He knelt down before her and gently removed her hands from her stomach. Then he kissed her, twice, on her belly button before getting back up and leaving the kitchen. Maisie's dress slipped back down over her stomach. Her own hands were left hanging in mid-air. When his lips touched the soft skin of her stomach she had felt the strange shivering start up again.

Winter. Cold and dank, but Myrtle Hughes's coughing fits seemed to have abruptly stopped. The Saturday after the kiss in the kitchen, Maisie had heard her coughing fit to burst. Then all had been quiet. Very quiet. The silence had continued all day Sunday. Mr Hughes did not come down into the parlour to eat any of his meals. He asked for them to be delivered up to his box bedroom. She hardly glimpsed him at all. He asked not to be disturbed. Her half-day was scheduled for Monday that week, but she had gone out reluctantly. The park was very cold. When she returned home, Mr Hughes was waiting in the hallway for her.

'My wife has died, Maisie. It was very sudden in the end. Shortly after you left the house. The doctor has been and he told me she suffered very little.'

'Will there be a funeral, sir?'

'On Wednesday. At her family home in Scunthorpe. I shall have to travel up.'

He left her then and went into the parlour. She heard him shut the door and that was that for the rest of the day. Maisie sat alone in the kitchen and wondered why everything felt so strange. She thought she might go and ask Mr Hughes whether he wanted something to eat, but he came into the kitchen and cancelled his own supper. He briefly pulled her to him, guiding her head to rest against his own stomach. He was what Maisie's mother would describe as 'on the portly side'. His belly was as soft as the bed in Zinc Street. Maisie burrowed up against him. Her hands found their way to his waist, which she squeezed as hard as she could in what she hoped was a sympathetic gesture. She felt clumsy touching him. Mr Hughes had caught up her hands after a few minutes and returned them to her lap.

'Sleep tight, dear heart. I have things to do.'

Then he was gone. Maisie felt his body heat still radiating across the kitchen. She hugged her arms across her chest and tried to imagine they were Mr Hughes' arms. She wanted to be held tight as she slept.

On the morning of Myrtle's funeral, Crawley disappeared out of the front door bearing two large suitcases. Returning home the following morning, he asked Maisie if she would like to go on holiday.

'I don't know, Crawley. I've never had a holiday before. Do you mean the seaside?'

Maisie pictured herself riding on a donkey, with Crawley at her side feeding her strawberries and cream. Her fifteenth birthday was just days away. Maybe they would celebrate by eating dinner in a hotel?

'No. A real holiday. We have to go on a ship. It's more of an adventure, Maisie. Something to help me forget the past.'

'I suppose so. Can I tell me mam?'

'Not necessary. We'll only be gone for a week or two. They can't miss you in that short space of time, now, can they?'

Maisie returned to the kitchen to prepare lunch. She was excited at the thought of sailing for the first time, but she was also worried. How was she going to pay for anything? She had spent nearly all her last wages on replacing her old winter shoes. And what did you wear on a boat? Crawley laughed off her worries.

'We shall make do, Maisie. In the meantime, it's an early night for both of us. Up with the lark to set sail from Fishguard.'

'It feels wicked. Going on holiday, seeing as how it will be washing day and everything.'

'Enjoy it, Maisie. It won't last long.'

It had lasted one day and one night. Maisie never got to have her holiday, because she was snatched up like a criminal and taken to the police station so fast she thought she might have dreamed Crawley's offer of a trip on a boat. But she didn't dream her mother's screams at the police station.

'You are a whore!'

'What, me, Mam?'

Maisie was stunned. She had been pole-axed a second time in the interview room when she was shown a newspaper's front-page story announcing the arrest of two people for the murder of Myrtle Hughes: 'The alleged murderer and his teenage paramour were going to make their escape by ship . . .'

She pleaded her innocence.

'I never did nothing, sirs. Nothing.'

The shame of it all, though, all the disappointment, all the confusion. His sleepy, hot hands still against her calico-white skin; his lips wet on her stomach; her face burning, the colour of a stolen apple. But Crawley Hughes had never made her lie down with him. Maisie wanted so much to tell people that, but she sensed their cynicism. They wanted to believe in the audacity of the murderer, who had dismembered his wife in the cellar as his 'paramour' cooked his tea in the kitchen above him. But he had sent her away on false missions. He had let her abandon him.

Maisie struggled with the truth, like she struggled with her aroused body, alone in a cell, lying on a plank of wood the width of the box-room bed. She bent over her stomach in the night and kissed it with all the passion she had been denied when the police had sealed a pair of handcuffs around her wrists. She had been torn from Crawley's side, clutching him so hard, her fingers had buried into the flesh on his shoulders. He had stood, dignified and very still, as she was carried away, screaming and biting at the strange hands which pawed at her twisting body. She screamed again when they said she was free to go. They admitted she was not an accessory to murder.

Maisie found the policemen's pity harder to stomach than their initial disgust at her.

Two weeks after her dramatic arrest, Maisie left Holloway prison with Crawley Hughes's pocket watch wrapped up in a brown paper parcel. He had sent it to her the day before he died on the gallows. Maisie had decided to keep it. She was going to make a new season begin with just a twist of her fingers. She was going to emigrate to Canada. Maisie set sail the spring she turned seventeen. Standing on the deck of the liner, she turned the hands of her gilt pocket watch forward.

Soon after arriving in Canada, she met and married a soldier called William Bolt. She gave him a false name and her virginity. She also gave him the pocket watch as a wedding present. Maisie felt very little several years later when she read the telegram explaining how her husband had been killed serving with his regiment in France. She simply noted the fact that Crawley would have been too old to have been called up. The pocket watch was returned to her rather belatedly by another soldier from her husband's regiment. She kept it pinned around her neck for another twenty years. It was a long time, long enough for most people to have forgotten the pale-faced girl who had kicked like an angry fish when poached away from her dreams. Maisie kept her husband's name and she had kept Crawley's watch, but she sold everything else in order to buy a small house on a new estate growing up on the outskirts of Cardiff. She was going home to Wales.

The seasons turned and Maisie kept up with them, turning the hands on the little watch. Old habits died hard, although so much else had disappeared from her life. She continued to break up sticks of green apple wood for her old-fashioned range and she soaked her nets in a copper outdoors. At night, she slept on a narrow metal bed under the stars. If she was cold, Maisie turned on her stomach and blew on the sheets to heat them, like she had done ever since she was a little girl. Maisie was always cold and she was always hungry. Even now she was grown up.

JEHANE MARKHAM

N e r u d a

Like pearls,
rubies, tin cans, bones, gold,
you left your words embedded on the page.

I could eat your poems
in a clutch
like a fox stealing eggs.

I offer you my treasure;
old roses
stone hands
newspaper faces
an urn of tears
my watercolour set.

Seated at the iron table
we might smile, exchange things.
Lift a dark yellow peach
or almonds from a bowl.

I sing to you
across the dark waters of the lake
I sing inside your death.
and your tenderness like an echo
comes singing back to rest.

L i l a c   b r e a t h

Lilac breath
(lost hope and the arms that once held me)
in a paradise of feelings
he lies across my breast
a little bag of bones
pulsating with hot secrets.
His serious succulent mouth
defies all fear of death.
With nonchalant love
he knuckles into my heart.
My kisses like pearls from deep within
are strung round and around his skin.

August

The quince tree stands
clapping the lemony rumps
between its dark green hands.

We pick the inky blackberries tangling over the path
watch out for shooting stars
play Monopoly on the hearth.

Time is a sigh, a breath,
like the wind catching the arms of the empty washing
I sense the coming of death.

The children make patterns out of desire,
their voices rising like smoke through the trees,
their destinies held by angels above the fire.

Insomnia

That old lady
with her cracked lampshades
her pools of red.
Her tick taking fingers pulse with the heat of despair.
As she pulls her needles
from the wool of counted sheep.
Sans shut eye
through the vaulty hours.

Inside the black bed
no sleep grows
only the inside crackle of thoughts
falling back to back
on the flattened pillow
into my hot ears
wired to the vanished light of day.

Smudges of orange glow
seep from the street
undermine the dark folds of night.
On the floor below
an old man coughs
and clears his throat against the dark and death
approaching on leathery paws like a stoat.

She cruises over the carpet
treading in the inky patterns
at the foot of the family bed.
Her broken eyebrows
her heartaches
the helter skelter of facts
in her uncombed hair.

In the top drawer
sleeping pills hum and bubble
among my underwear.
Little fisheye lead me out of trouble
to a place of shadows
a sweet fall
where my lover is dead in his snores
his hot arms holding dreams.

In the swampy waters of dawn
she's still at me
sucking my blood
into a thumb of leach.
She worms her way
under my skin.
She's alive with worry.

Old lady, shut your fat handbag and go!
Take your private smells
lipstick and crumbs
cellophane veils.
Take your heavy head
and go down into the deep.

When you're gone
there's such a quietness in the room
as if the sea was stuffed and hung.
Seahorses,
limpets and suckers on the swell
drifting my bones to sleep.

Wild cards

It's the fuckers I like the most. The ones who want a straight-forward fuck. No added frills. No suck my dick or let me eat your pussy or weird spanking shit. They give me the money up front, I take them to my room and when the deed's done they walk away and everyone's happy. I'm richer, they're poorer, a million or more wasted sperm flushed away in a used rubber wrap.

I don't want children. I've never wanted children. There's already too many people crowding this planet, eating up the empty spaces like empty spaces are infinite. As far as I can see, Britain's turning into one huge, fucking housing estate. When I've got enough money together, I'm getting on to a plane and leaving. I've chosen America. It's not perfect, but where is? At least they've got stretches of land as large as this country with no people, no roads, nothing but trees and sky and wild animals that are still wild and animal enough to eat you.

I'm in the bloody business because it pays. No taxes, no NI

stamp, just pure profit. I was on the dole for a year but that wasn't getting me anywhere. So I got off my ass and decided to sell the one thing I was born with. It's good being self-employed. I'm in control and there's no one to answer to. It's not easy keeping the pimps at bay: no man with a mean mind likes a woman doing her own thing. But I've got plenty of brass neck and a Swiss army knife; I'd slit their throats if I had to.

It's an art, living this way. I'm like two people inside the same skin. Not even the punters recognise me when I'm having time off; walking down the street, standing in a supermarket queue, buying a glass of wine in a bar. They walk right past me, holding their wife's hand or their daughter's hand and I'm thinking, if only they knew. Knew how many times he's called me Mummy, or Bitch, or Baby.

Comfort is the fact that every fuck brings me an air mile closer to America.

Friday night and I'm out. Tight black skirt and velvet top scooped low. White musk scent. I need money tonight. This week's been slow and I've spent everything I've earned on food and a new pair of jeans. I don't have to wait long. A car turns the corner and I will it to stop. The man winds down his window, throws me a look. I sidle up to him, taking my time. Being on the game's a game of tactics; if you're too keen they don't like it.

'Joey,' he says.

'Don't know anyone called that,' I say.

'No,' he says, 'I'm Joey.'

No punter's ever introduced himself before. It's safer that way. And more exciting; anonymity adds an edge, helps them give voice to secret fantasies. I'm off guard with this man from the start: he's played a wild card and thrown me. He nods to the passenger door and I get in.

'I want sex outside,' he says.

'I don't do that,' I say.

'I'll make it worth your while,' he says.

I shake my head. Watch him rub his hands together, turning them over and looking at the smooth, pink palms.

'I work for the council,' he says. 'I spend all day, every day cooped up like a chicken.'

'So?' I say.

He lights a cigarette. Draws deep. Clouds the car with smoke.

'So I'm going insane.'

'Tough,' I say.

'I'll make a deal with you,' he says.

'I don't make deals,' I say. 'Twenty pounds for a fuck, fifteen for a blow job and that's it.'

He looks at me, puts his hand on my knee.

'Please?' he says.

'My room or nowhere,' I say. But already I'm thinking, how much would he pay me?

I only trade in my strip-lit room just off Stoke's Croft. There's a phone next to the bed. A sink down the hall where they can wash themselves off before as well as after. My room, my rules, these four walls are the closest I come to insuring my life. They're solid and if any fucker tries something on I know where the door is and there are people near enough to hear me shouting.

He stubs his cigarette out. The two of us sitting in the car like dummies. I see other cars cruising by. Every minute here is money lost, but I don't move. There's something about him, and I know already that I'm about to make a foolish decision.

'Sixty pounds,' he says. 'I'll pay you sixty pounds.'

'Eighty,' I say.

'Seventy?'

'Eighty.'

He starts the engine and we pull away. I put on my seat belt, and laugh at myself. As if that can save me.

Stupid, stupid, stupid, I'm saying to myself all the way across the city and over the suspension bridge. Stupid fucker, letting yourself be driven through the gates of Ashton Court and into the dark. And Christ, it's dark. Black trees and black sky with just the sharp blade of headlights pointing ahead. Adrenaline pumping through me so that I have to sit on my hands to stop them from shaking. He's taking me to the sort of place where somebody, some innocent dog-walker, will be out innocently walking their dog one day and find my body rotting in the undergrowth.

He doesn't talk and I don't talk. We get out of the car and start walking. I want to turn and run. Run back to the city. The oasis of orange light shimmering in the distance. But I don't. I follow him across the golf course. Take off my shoes because the heels spike into the mud and slow me down.

A few trees into the wood he stops. We lie down. I take off my pants and he gets on top of me. Then he rolls over so I'm on top of him. He's soft. I slide down between his legs, but nothing stirs.

'I've never done anything like this before,' he says.

'Don't worry about it,' I say. They always act as if they're disappointing me in some way when they can't get it up. I don't give a fuck, I want to say, but I'm biting my tongue with this one. I don't want his wounded pride wounded any more. I want to keep him sweet because I want to get back to the house in one piece.

'Can we just lie here for a while?' he says.

'Whatever.'

There are twigs digging into my back and I'm freezing.

'Can you hear the trees laughing?' he says.

'What?'

'Listen,' he says: 'the wind in the trees, tickling the leaves and making them laugh.'

This is the craziest non-fuck I've ever had. A punter paying me to lie in the woods and think poetic thoughts. I rub my arms. My fingers are blue. He takes my hand and licks it. Opens my legs with his knee. Hard as a rock this time, he squeezes his way in, saying 'I don't want to hurt you,' but hurting me all the same as he rams away and I'm dry and tight and thinking eighty pounds closer, eighty pounds closer to my flight. At least he comes quickly. Small blessing. Then he's leaning over me and looking in my eyes. His face blue with the post-fuck blues; I see it on every man's face after they've come. The sudden, bleak realisation that nothing's changed, that they haven't been sent shooting up to heaven after all.

'Thank you,' he says.

'What?' I say, because even though he hasn't killed me yet I feel as if I'm freezing to death.

'Thank you.'

Then he's reaching into his pocket and pulling out his wallet. He hands me one fifty-pound note and three tens. Crisp and new. I take them and shove them inside my bra. Stand up and start walking away. He follows, a few steps behind, his deep breathing kneading into my neck with its soft, rasping sound.

He drives me back to the city and drops me off where he picked me up. I'm almost delirious about the fact that I'm still alive. Still breathing, I go to Rita's and order cod and chips and mushy peas. Take them home and savour every mouthful. Swear to myself that I'll never take a risk like that again.

Days pass in a blur of sex and routine. One man who likes my hands tight around his throat, his prick wedged between my thighs. Another who wanted to fuck me in the ass but made do with a blow job. Taking my sheets to the launderette and watching them turn in the machine, suds scummed with spunk and lubrication cream. Phoning my mum, telling her about my work as a waitress and the fantastic tips I've been getting lately. My mum said once, perhaps I should try doing what you do, to supplement my pension. I changed the subject quickly; the thought of her lying beneath a thousand strangers turned my stomach.

Then, a week to the day we first met, Joey turns up again. Surprises me again. I had him down for a one-offer, a man who made a mistake and went running back to his wife.

'What do you want?' I say to him.

'The same again,' he says.

'The price has gone up,' I say.

'Whatever,' he says.

And then I'm in the car, breaking my promise to myself, flooding with the same thoughts as before. This is too dangerous, this is stupid, this is good money. He's wearing a different aftershave this time. It's slightly bitter, leaves a lemony taste on my tongue when I breathe.

'Why me?' I ask him. 'You could have anyone else for half the price.'

'I don't want anyone else,' he says.

'Why not?'

He shrugs his shoulders.

He's brought a blanket and a bottle of wine with him this time. The blanket's good, but I don't drink when I'm at work. He toasts the moon and drinks straight from the bottle. Then he says, 'Tickle me.'

So I tickle him and he starts to giggle.

'When I was a kid,' he says, 'my mother forbade tickling. She said it would make me piss my pants or stutter when I grew up.'

'Really?' I say.

Then he undresses me, slowly, peeling away my clothes. He starts to lick me – my thighs, my belly, my breasts. He goes to bury his head between my legs but he isn't a man who wants to eat pussy, he's a man who's trying to turn me on.

'Stop,' I say.

'Why?' he says.

'It's not what we're here for,' I say, and I mean it. 'Work is work and I want to keep it that way.' Be able to keep the doors inside of me closed. Protect myself like any other professional: surgeon, pathologist, professor.

'Suit yourself,' he says, rolling on the rubber while I smother myself in cream.

I watch him as he pumps away. He's quite good-looking, really. Thick black hair and deep-set eyes. A scar on his left cheek that makes him look as if he's always smiling.

'What's your name?' he says.

'Angelita,' I say.

'Angelita,' he says, rolling the word around in his mouth as if it means everything to him. It's not my real name. I don't want them getting inside of me. Not even an inch inside.

'How old are you?' he says.

'Enough fucking questions,' I say. 'Just get on with it.'

'I was just asking, that's all,' he says.

'Well don't. You buy my body, not my mind.'

He doesn't come tonight. He gives up halfway through, withdraws and reaches for the wine. His mind's somewhere else.

'Do you know,' he says, pointing at the moon, 'that if you were to run across the moon's surface at ten Ks an hour, you could see the sun rising for ever?'

'No,' I say.

'It's true,' he says.

'Really,' I say.

'Do you care about me?' he says.

'No,' I say.

He doesn't like that. 'Well, I care about you.'

'You're paying,' I say, 'so you can do whatever you want.'

'Tell me you love me,' he says.

'I love you.'

'Mean it,' he says. He's leaning over me again. Gulping down the wine, spilling it on his chin and shirt. 'For fuck's sake I want you to mean it.' He's getting drunk. The wine is wending its way around his tense body and making him feel bigger than he is. I don't like him like this.

'I love you,' I say, as softly, as gently, as meaningfully as I can.

'You don't fucking mean that!' he screams. Then he's standing up, waving the bottle in the air, smashing it against the nearest tree.

But I'm not listening any more. I'm up on my feet and running. Heart beating hard and fast in my chest and the only thing I can think is I don't want to die. Not like this. Not here. But he's faster than me. I can hear him behind, shouting for me to come back, shouting Angelita, Angelita, and I'm praying as hard as I'm running but it doesn't make any difference. He catches me up and grabs my arm.

'Let me go!' I say. 'You've got what you paid for.'

But he won't let me go. A mad look in his bloodshot eyes, one hand on my arm, the other holding the broken bottle neck.

'You fool,' he says. I scratch my nails down his face and kick him, but he still won't let go. Then he's slicing at his skin with the glass. Slicing his arm until it's red and dripping with blood.

I stop fighting for a moment and look at him.

'It's not you I want to hurt,' he says, 'it's me. Me!'

'Jesus,' I say, because he's shaking and sobbing and down on his knees. Kneeling in front of me as if he's at church waiting for his wafer and wine.

'I'm not your fucking Madonna!' I scream because I hate him for scaring me like that.

'I'm sorry,' he says, 'I'm sorry.'

It's a long walk back to the city but I don't care. My arm is bruised and sore and my head is spinning. Everything is suddenly loud. The cars, people's voices, loud, all too loud. I take back streets because they're quieter and I think he won't find me here. He won't be able to follow me here.

I'm wrong.

I can hear the chug and churn of his diesel engine. Then he's alongside me, driving slowly, leaning over and winding the passenger window down.

'Get in,' he says.

I cross the road.

He stops the car, gets out, follows. 'I just want to talk to you,' he says.

I walk faster and faster, but he keeps up with me.

'My son,' he says, as if that means anything to me. 'A year ago today,' he says, struggling to get the words out. 'Died.'

'So what?' I say.

'So I don't know what to do with how I feel.'

I turn to face him. 'I'm a prostitute, not a counsellor,' I say.

'Yes,' he says, 'but I know you understand.'

That sends a shiver through me. Makes me stop. Makes me turn to look at him. 'What the fuck makes you think that?' I say.

'It's written all over you,' he says.

'What is?'

'Grief,' he says.

'Crap,' I say.

'So you've never felt pain?' he says.

That makes me laugh. That's the whole point, I want to tell him. I've felt so much fucking pain in my life that the last thing I need is to feel someone else's. But by now there's a crowd gathering. Watching us. Watching a man in a suit with his arm bleeding and a woman whose feet and legs are covered in mud. Both shouting and swearing at each other in a part of the city where shouting and swearing only happens behind closed doors. I'm worried someone might call the police. I walk back to the car and he follows.

'Drive,' I say.

'Where?' he says.

'Anyfuckingwhere.'

He starts the engine and speeds away.

We circle the city in silence. Joey's face is white. I don't know what he's got over me, this one, but I can feel myself giving in. The softer side of me being drawn out by his pain. I hate myself for it, but there's nothing I can do. I direct him to my room on

Stoke's Croft. We climb the stairs and go inside. He takes off his jacket and shirt while I fetch warm water and cotton wool. He winces as I bathe the cut.

'You should get stitches,' I say.

'No need,' he says. 'I heal quickly.' Then he laughs at himself.

I rip up an old T-shirt that's lying on the bed and wrap it around the wound.

'A motorbike accident,' he says. 'A car wasn't looking before it turned the corner. He died instantly.' He hesitates, then carries on. 'I thought I was all right. Thought I was handling it well. But every now and then these feelings well up inside of me and I don't know what to do.'

'Feel them,' I say.

That starts him off again. Crying. Wiping the tears from his face with the back of his hand. 'You know the one thing I can't get out of my mind?' he says.

'No.'

'We signed a consent form for organ donation and I wish we hadn't. I wish we'd buried him whole. Every time I picture him in my mind now, there are pieces of him missing.' Joey shudders. Takes a deep breath and looks at his watch. 'Can I see you again?' he says.

No, I think. 'Yes,' I say.

'I want to take you to the beach,' he says. 'Next week.'

No, I think again. 'OK,' I say.

'Tuesday?'

'Wednesday.'

He puts on his shirt and jacket and heads for the door. Looks over his shoulder at me before leaving.

I crawl across the floor on my hands and knees, curl up in front of the radiator. She's here again. He's brought her back and I hate him for it. I can see her face every time I close my eyes. I can feel the cramps in my belly and the blood on my legs as if it's happening all over again. My baby. The little girl I gave birth to when I was fifteen years old. She had arms like flippers and a head the size of a football. That's what comes of being fucked by your father, I wanted to say. But I didn't. I pull my knees into my chest but I can't stop the tears. Burning down my face. 'Stop this,' I whisper; 'stop this now.' I get up. Drag a comb through my hair and put on make-up. Brush the mud off my shoes and legs and head out into the streets. I want to be meat again.

I work ten men that night. Work until I'm so exhausted I fall into bed and sleep dreamless.

The next afternoon the sun is shining bright in my room. It almost makes me happy. I take a long bath and eat pasta with olives and tomatoes. Watch television, get bored, read a book instead. Disappear inside my head, inside a world that's pure fucking fiction. There's nothing else like it. That's what I'm going to do in America. Hole myself up for a few months with a library of good books and read and read until I'm so fat with reading I won't be able to take another word in. I check my bank book and I've got two and a half thousand pounds. It's enough, but I want more. Want to live like a queen for a while. One thousand more, I think, then I'll be ready.

Wednesday comes too quickly. I don't know what I'm getting myself into with Joey. I can feel myself liking him and I don't want that. It's dangerous. It's not what I'm in this for.

He knocks on my door at 11.15. 'Weston-super-Mare,' he says.

'Two hundred pounds,' I say.

He smiles and takes out his wallet. Counts one hundred and thirty pounds into my hand, says he'll give me the rest later. I put the money in a tin, put on a coat, then go out to his car.

He parks on the front. Even though it's a cold March day, people are lounging on the sand behind windbreaks. Joey takes my hand and we walk along the sand to a canopied stall near the pier. I try on a pair of mirror sunglasses and put combs edged with tiny pink shells in my hair. I'm trying to have fun. Joey drags me over to another stall where he spends ages deciding if he wants winkles or whelks or crab sticks. In the end he goes for a mixture, then remembers that he hasn't got any money. We run away, giggling.

We go past arcades and fish and chip shops until Joey spies a bank. I stand next to him as he pushes in his card and types his secret number. The sun sneaks out from behind a cloud. We take a tiny electric train to the arcade at the end of the pier. Play push-penny with 2ps. Win some, lose more. Joey tries to capture a yellow duck, but the hook drops it just before it reaches the hatch. Then he has a go on a skiing machine. His virtual self crashes into a fence and somersaults in the air.

The tide comes in. Quietly. Lifting beached boats off their hulls, juggling them on waves. We buy tea in plastic cups and drink it on the beach. Six nuns walk along the shoreline, holding their sandals in their hands. One of them splashes about in the waves, wetting the hem of her habit. Joey leans towards me. Jesus, I think, not now. He kisses me then pushes me on to my back.

'Not yet,' I say, nodding in the direction of the nuns.

'I just wanted to kiss you,' he says, looking hurt.

'Baby,' I say, 'I didn't mean to upset you.' I stroke his face.

He softens. Looks pleased with himself. Thinking he's got me exactly where he wants me.

'I meant what I said the other night,' he says, 'about loving you.'

'What about your wife?' I say, mixing equal amounts of jealousy with tenderness.

'Since our son died she's disappeared inside herself. I can't reach her any more.'

I let him put his arm around me as we walk along. I even put my arm around his waist and pinch him gently. He likes that. Likes the way I rest my head on his shoulder. Whispering little intimacies in his ear. 'You're different, Joey. From all the rest. I like you, Joey. I love you, Joey. I want to be yours, Joey, only yours.'

We check into a hotel, kiss in the lift, kiss in the corridor; he's so hot he can hardly wait to get me in the room and out of my clothes. We make love, have sex, until I'm sure he's exhausted; fucked to the point where all he can do is sleep. Deep. Very, very deep. I wait and I watch. His breathing changes and I know he's sinking. I call his name and he groans but he doesn't wake.

There is not a single second to be wasted.

I slide out of the bed and dress. Take the wallet from his jacket, car keys from his trousers. I skip down the spiralling stairs chanting his PIN number in my head. About to deal Joey a wild card of my own.

HELEN FARISH

Do that again

I want everything to stay as it is,
nothing to be moved, cleaned away.
Your coffee cup with the saucer dribble,
a lipstick on the floor. My T-shirt
on the dining-room table, the smear of your mouth
which must also be the smear of my sex
on the orange juice glass. Take nothing back
to how it was. Leave the sheets
smelling of you, your hair
on the pillow. Leave my mouth
sore. And leave those glasses in the pubs
that measured our day till the Angel and Greyhound
could keep us apart no longer,
till I had to kiss you, had to,
till I heard you say Do *that again*.

Till I did it again and again, till nothing
was held back, everything
moved and only a smear left
of what went before.

Moved by wolves

The she-wolf tracked her mate beyond
their territory, followed his scent
to the grass blade, down from the hills
into low lying land with a certainty
that was stunning, without a single
change in pace nor a whiff of doubt.

He was her highway, her freeway
and she travelled him 300 miles
even though he'd left without her;
arrived like a silent train to find him.
Then a tabloid farmer from a safe distance
shot her. Paid no fine.

My food practically afloat I abandon
attempts to eat, taken aback
by wolves tracking me all the way
from North America to my living room,
transforming my face to how it looked
two years ago.

730 days blade to blade it's been
his scent before and behind, finding me even here
in the room I painted to throw him off.
How many years does it take to put a safe
distance between us? Years of dinners floating
because of him and me and wolves.

Yukiko the plate

I am a plate. Chopsticks
prod me, fish stains
my skin with stink.

To test me for my plateness they placed
six eggs on my body and for four hours
dropped ice cubes. Each time I flinched
the timer was set back to nought.

Now four men in fat robes pay
£700 to eat sushi off me. How they love
the morsels from my genitals;
they never know whether
to start there or work their way up
from thigh and belly, the fluted edges.

This body which is a plate, which has been
waxed and shaven, rubbed with
scentless soap, with bags of bran,
scrubbed with loofahs, hot water
cold water. This plate which must have
no scent of its own. Which is
laid on rush mats, the hair fanned out, petalled.

What do I feel when I get up and walk
knowing that chopsticks have been in my genitals,
that vomit has soaked my skin, that their comments

cling to me like the stink of squid or scallops?
I want to break into sharp pieces, use them to stab
fishermen, restaurant owners, chefs, diners,
businessmen, fathers, brothers, sons, economists;

the producers of lime juice and rock salt
who set the price so high
for taking away the smell.

Twenty-four days

I'm not reading. I'm thinking about
your hands, all the things they must have
held, like train doors, coffee cups,
thoughts.
          Clean nails, the bones
like a ballerina's.

Like someone you might start loving
quickly without knowing why
except that he said Christ
when a lemon got in his mouth,
except that he was wearing
stocking feet, that his hair
was a Red Indian's and his eyes
left the European behind.

That all the time you knew him a river ran
and the only thing to stop it
on the twenty-third day was his face
held in the courtyard like a reservoir
of happiness. Love swelled,
glinted like the underside
of a white bird floating on
the surface of sunlight as though it were
textured. And Christ I was moved.

His face held there while the waters
banked up, while the castle lost
a split second of its history, while I lost
that promise I had made to myself.

The river ran on, the train door slammed
and a woman already in love with him checked
the time of arrival.

SARAH VAN HOVE

All in a moment

Liz ran the bath and felt the water to make sure it was the right temperature, just as she always had for her own children. The bath ritual brought them back as vividly as if they were standing in front of her. Their thin, lithe, perfect bodies shivering and complaining and clamouring for attention. When they were little she had taken them on her lap and enveloped them in large soft towels and sang to them. Now they locked the door and wouldn't let her in. When she called they could not hear above the loud heavy blare of the radio. They spent ages in there. Washing their hair. Using all the hot water. Leaving the place a tip.

Now it was her mother standing helplessly in front of her. A baby could be cherished precisely because of its dependence. A mother ought to know better. Arms up, jersey over the head, buttons, zip, skirt down, tights off; slowly does it. There were such a lot of layers. It was simple if you knew what you were doing. If not, it was terrible. Anything could go on top of anything. There were infinite combinations. A terrifying tangle of garments of all different shapes and sizes. A book of pre-supposed knowledge that you could not read any more.

Liz stopped for a moment and stared out of the bathroom window. The moors stretched towards the sky. Sheep dotted the field in front of the house. The road led up towards the gate. She had seen it hundreds of times. What if it wasn't like that? What if the sheep were stones like her mother had told her yesterday? Who was to say? She gripped the basin as if trying to hold on to reality. Once that slipped, everything went. Nothing was certain. The world was no longer safe. Cows were crocodiles waiting to pounce. Sausages were snakes. Pills were poison. She glimpsed for a moment the fear in which her mother lived. She shuddered. If you lost your memory you lost yourself. If you forgot who you were, then you could be anyone. The possibilities were endless. There were no limits. Madness was nothing more than a moment away.

'How clever you are,' her mother had said at supper, as Liz had cut up her tomatoes for her, 'knowing all this.' Her mother was adamant she had never seen a tomato before in her life. She had no idea what to do with it. Liz had watched the tomato shed its name in front of her and become a slushy ball of pips and skin. We are all disintegrating, she thought desperately. Sanity was fragile. She must be strong. Her mother was waiting for her bath. They couldn't both go under.

Grace stood outside her body and watched this girl who was as familiar as her own shadow and yet as much a stranger as she was to herself. She fiddled and fumbled and pulled things on and off and her skin stretched and shook and sighed. She had felt warm and cosy before. Now she was cold and shivering. There were little pimples on her arms. If she took off another layer she would be down to her bones. They felt as brittle as a ginger biscuit.

Now this girl was holding her, tightly forcing her forward. She must take a step. Into this huge white basin. There had been something like this before in another part of the room.

She looked desperately round but it seemed to have gone. This was built for a giant. She did not know if she would be able to get into it. Or what she would find there.

On the other side it was warm and wet and she was sitting in it. She smiled in relief. The girl was talking to her. Loud and slow as if she was a deaf child. It seemed she was somewhere very far off, as if there was an ocean between them. She heard her and yet her words whisked themselves away in the wind and she could not catch them. They slipped through her fingers like this soft squidgy thing that the girl had placed in her hand. She wondered if it was something to eat. 'Wash yourself with it, Mum,' said Liz in exasperation. She leaned over and tried to show her.

Liz wanted to get her mother to lie back and relax. Sometimes when she observed her thin wizened body she felt such a stab of love and pity that it was like a physical jab of pain. Round her bottom her skin seemed like it was about to fall off. On her shoulders and elbows and round her neck it barely covered her bones that jutted out, angular and uncomfortable. Her stomach was loose and flat as if all life had been sucked out of it. How could she ever have carried her in that empty concave hollow? Once it must have been full and ripe and waiting to bring forth life. Not just her but Sean and Thomas and Mark.

We cease to be fertile. We shed our selves. Slowly and sorely until there is nothing left but skin and bones. Would her daughters do the same thing for her as she was doing now to her mother? Would they nurse these thoughts? Or would they believe it could never happen to them? That was the strength and beauty of youth. The certainty. The sufficiency of the moment. Her mother's breasts sagged sadly as if there was no use for them any more. She had little pubic hair left. There was nothing to cover or hide.

It was like the body of a little, old child.

Her mother had discovered her toes. She wiggled them in the water, enjoying the sound of the splash and the feel of the warmth between them. She looked up and smiled. Liz tried to smile back. She wished she could enter into this world of discovery where everything was for the first time and share in her mother's sense of wonder. But she couldn't. She stood fiercely on the outside, staring coldly. There was a dribble on her mother's chin and a piece of squashed tomato from supper lodged precariously at the corner of her mouth. The sight of her large pale toes splashing in the water was an uncomfortable one for her daughter. She could not delight in this old baby. She did not want a new child at this stage in her life. She wanted her mother. As she had known her. Not as she was now. She wanted to go back and bury her head in her skirt like she had as a little girl and for her mother to tell her that it wasn't true. It was only a fairy tale. It didn't matter. It was only a plate. They could glue it together. But it was too late for that. There wasn't a happy ending. It couldn't be mended. Her mother's mind was broken.

'It's time to get you out,' said Liz briskly. Suddenly she couldn't stand the sight of her mother so bare and babyish yet without the hope and potential that went with a real baby.

Grace did not want to leave the warm well of the water. She had no wish to be manhandled again. She would like to have wafted into warmth and comfort and companionship. Instead this girl was commanding her like a military officer.

Liz shouted into her mother's eyes. 'It's time to get out. *Out*. You have to stand up.' The words spat like bullets. Grace's face blotted into bewilderment. Liz leaned over and placed her mother's arms firmly on both sides of the bath. Her grip hurt. Then she heaved Grace up from behind. She toppled slightly but managed to steady herself against the cold rim of the bath. 'There we go,' Liz said like a cross, tired nurse to a fractious baby. 'Step out now.' Her mother didn't know which leg to move first. She asked Liz tentatively which she thought would be best. 'This one,' said Liz, pointing to the one nearest the side. Grace tried. It hardly moved. Perhaps the other would be better. Or both. It was like a cage she was contained in. How would she ever get out of it? She felt trapped. Her eyes darted fearfully from left to right like a hunted animal but she saw no escape. The trap was tight and gave little room for manoeuvre. She closed her eyes for a moment. She would have liked to climb out of her body and run like the wind. She felt herself slip, only to be carried by the strong arms of this angry soldier.

'What the hell are you doing?' shouted Liz crossly. 'Put one leg out and then the other.'

She held her mother's thin arms in her strong angry hands while she made an elaborate performance of the perfectly ordinary procedure of getting out of the bath. I should be feeling sorry, thought Liz helplessly and instead I'm so angry. I hate her frailty. I hate the way she has forgotten the simplest of things. I hate the absurdity of it all. She dried her roughly with the slightly damp towel. Grace flinched. Liz knew she was being harsh. She couldn't seem to stop herself. Anger welled within and fed itself on every indication of feebleness. She put the nightie over Grace's head and pulled it down. A wisp of hair caught on a hook and was yanked free. When she came to do up the buttons she felt the force in her fingers itching to push her to the ground. When she squeezed Grace's arm through her sleeve she had to stop herself from squeezing her to death.

Liz squashed her mother's knobbly feet into her faded, worn-down tartan slippers. Tears smarted in her eyes at the bumpy swollen contours of her feet. The poignancy of those old slippers almost made her choke. What she was doing appalled her. Yet anger had taken hold and was not to be beaten. The weakness of her mother increased her strength. She made her go to the lavatory. When nothing happened she pushed her back down to try again. The sight of her mother's bony fingers pressing a too small square of tissue paper between her legs filled her with disgust. She gritted her teeth and turned stiffly away. Her whole body was shaking.

She bundled her down the passage and into bed. Grace was meek and compliant now as if sensing the futility of rising against such a hurricane. Liz snapped off the light and said goodnight in a loud, unnatural voice that didn't belong to her. She pulled the door to in relief. Almost at once the storm subsided, leaving an aching void. Don't let her remember, she pleaded desperately. Make her forget. She buried her face in her hands in despair.

That was the problem. It's all there. Somewhere. It's just not in the right order any more.

The softness of the blanket pulled gently over a sleeping child to keep her warm. The hard rough hand of a daughter against the wrinkled body of an old mother. The beginning and the end. The end and the beginning. Everything we have ever done. It's a part of us. We cannot forget.

She cleaned up the bathroom, silent and subdued. The memory of what had happened stained her hands and pricked her eyes. She scrubbed at the bath. She could not get rid of it. She wiped the smudge of toothpaste off the mirror. She stared at herself. I don't like what I see, she thought. But I can't get away from it. I can't escape. She swallowed and found the different parts of herself hard to digest. They stuck in her throat and made her choke.

She put the kettle on for a cup of tea. She chose her mother's mug with care. She would make sure there was plenty of milk. That it wasn't too hot. That there were two level teaspoons of sugar, well stirred. She applied herself to this fierce attention to detail as if her life depended on it. It was as if in this cup of tea she placed all her love for her mother. She noticed with chagrin that the cup was chipped.

She took a sip to make sure it was not too hot and carried it carefully along the lighted corridor to her room. She didn't want to spill a single drop. She opened the door gently and found the bed was empty. Her mother had disappeared.

Grace had slipped out of her body and hung it on a hook by the door. It was a beautiful day.

The magnolia was in blossom. At the far end of the garden was a swing. She was watching her children. They had tumbled one after another out of her and into the world. She had never had any problems with childbearing. She felt she could have gone on for ever but four was enough for William. 'There's no space for me any more,' he complained as four tiny bodies burrowed themselves into their bed in the early morning and he lay there in his striped pyjamas longing to have her to himself. The youngest was a girl. She had always wanted a daughter. She was swinging high up into the leaves. She was almost part of the sky. Grace's face clouded over for a moment. She called into the clouds. 'Careful now, Liz. Not too high!' but the words were blown away by the wind.

She picked her way down the path. Lavender filled the air. She always loved spring the best. Every year it returned without fail. Sean was coming towards her on his tricycle. His fair curly hair flopped over his eyes. His face was streaked with dirt. He careered towards her and the wheels hit a stone and the tractor turned and he was lying on the ground howling. She picked him up. He was as light as a feather. 'Where does it hurt?' she asked. He rubbed his nose and pointed to the scratched scrubbed surface of his knee. 'I'll kiss it better.' She always could. He raced off along the path. She was a conjuror. Comforter. Everything they needed. It was all there in that moment in the garden.

She heard her daughter calling to her through the apple blossom. 'Mum! Mummee! I can fly!' And she was. Soaring above her, spiralling into the sun and back. Fearless. Loved. She waved. She hoped Will had secured the swing. There was a crack. A screeching of something overhead. And then she was running towards her. Crumpled on the ground. A tiny tangle of limbs and ligaments. Blood on her yellow dress. Fear in her dark eyes.

'Mum. There you are. I didn't know where you'd got to.' Grace was crouched down in front of the flowerbed, her nightie hanging loosely off her shoulders. She was murmuring to herself. Liz knelt down beside her. 'I was worried. You shouldn't be out here. You'll catch your death of cold.'

Her mother stared at her. The little girl had gone. She must have been all right. Just the shock. And a broken nose. She stared at this tall woman bending down in front of her. She seemed to be crying. 'I'm sorry, Mum. I get so cross. I'm a terrible daughter.'

Daughter? Grace's forehead furrowed as if delving back into the wrinkles of history. Then it loosened. A softness spread over her. 'I told her not to go so high,' she said as if confiding in a stranger. 'But she wanted to fly. Through the trees. She was always one for doing her own thing. I had sons too. Lovely boys. I couldn't have hoped for better children.' She smiled and the mist lifted. She peered at the face in front of her. That was it. 'Elizabeth. We always called her Liz.' She stared at her for a moment and then squeezed her hand. 'Funny thing is, you remind me of her somehow.' Liz draped the dressing gown round her mother's bony shoulders and led her gently inside.

ABI HUGHES-EDWARDS

After Heaven: Mephistopheles' walking tour

I am falling through small towns
where fathers sleep with daughters
and wash cars on Sunday afternoons.
Around the towns, countryside. Sympathetic lines
of rise, stick and plundered barrow, optical gilt
on the far ends of narrowed heights of streets
with pavements bruised from Saturday nights
of rise, stick and harrow, oh guilty receptacle
'Five months and still not showing, pet?'

I have fallen through the arse of this town
and am leaving with the bells shaking
the camphor from best skirts and coats.

Deeply discordant bells, probably a tape recording
to save the shaky phallus of precious Saxon church.
I know it's melodramatic, as corny as no shadow, sudden fog,
but I can't resist browning the yews as I pass,
smiling at a girl, enough in His image to still tempt her heart.
Thank you Mrs Vaughn-Williams for your bedsit,
the carbon monoxide optional extra front room,
which you said was a little piece of Heaven. I agreed.
Mine has shrunk to a lockable door, far removed
from all that eternal light and fraternal fluttering of wings.

I've quite fallen for smalltown sleaze,
their inland pig roasts and petty crime sprees,
the sixties shop fronts, the violence behind the new UPVC.

Along the coast you can follow the smell of fish and tripper
to streets of damp newspaper and crab claws,
fairgrounds dangerous with gull shit.
They are all the same and in between, the tired space
where I pause to pass a night. All dark to you
but my sight, infrared, salvaged from the old days,
traces the bloodsport of foxes, the suck of stoat,
the fading warmth in newly dug soil.
Another corner of a local field that is for ever.

I won't be the fall guy for the husbands, their clumsy sons
so I always move on in the jangle of the early morning.
Sometimes benevolent, leaving in languid pungent circles
before the tracker curs come to cringe over my prints.
Hey nonny nonny, the family of man, Heaven on earth.

At the boarding house for ailing priests
my arrival has turned the bracing air to sea-cloud
mists as insidious as distilled snake hiss,
restful after the south's disturbing currents.
I've taken the cloth, a matter for tailors,
and called myself Michael; we were friends once,
I know he'll mind.

In this boarding house the wallpaper
is lifted annually by the emphysemic wheezings
of convalescent priests, marooned in the parlour,
pegged out carrion-style in the sun lounge.
There are rosaries on every bedside table
like a pattern of cockroaches beside the Gideon.
The ice cream is served without wafers.

I am spoilt, pitied as one relatively young,
unblemished in this companionship of cirrhosis, cancer,
adulterous disbelievers and, of course, pederasts praying.
'Another helping, Father Michael?' asks the girl,
full of unholy feeling when I just need to relax.
Let her take her masturbations to that
listening coffin full of desiccated man.

At night the house murmurs with conscience
and the clicking of beads like a usurer's abacus.
The noise dies down until that 4 a.m.
irregularity of heart and breath.
An urgent bell comes sharp tapping on my door:

'Father Michael, Father Michael,
Father James is taken terrible bad.'
I step naked from the bed before she can turn
and follow her blush down the Madonna'd corridor.

Father James sleeps on necessary polythene
as loud as crisp packets, his whimpering voice
like an SOS against the crackle.
I tune in and listen to a confession
as mucky as a wet fart, as interesting
as a drying stain until he retches
into the bucket and frightens the name 'Davie' out.

Suddenly I make that leap of faith
and know his Davie, the gap-toothed, the freckled,
you know the clichés; it was the same Davie:
no rubbers a tenner extra at the back of Bristol station.
Oh Father James who caned catechisms into bare boys
there'll be no circles of white light to hurt my eyes.
Let me kiss you Father, for you have sinned.

Incense thick as phlegm follows me as I leave
and the girl, sullen in her niche
of maddened Spanish plaster, watches.
I strike out along the coast road;
fog in front, blue breaking behind.

My little pony

Not yesterday, not the day before but the day before, Mummy was in the kitchen when I came down! Not still in bed. She was sitting at the table waiting for me, just like Christmas morning. Only she was watching the apple tree, or the grass, or something. I'm too small to see. Watching really hard, so she didn't hear me.

'Boo!'

It started off being my favourite day since Christmas Day.

'Your arms look sad!' I joked. They were dangling as limp as my Ragamuffin doll's. I pulled myself on to her knee and wrapped her sad arms around me. Her face came down and fluffed in the hair on top of my head. Now I could see she'd been watching the wind: apple-blossom swirling in the yard; a fertiliser bag up in the air like a kite. After cuddling her, I said, 'Mummy, can I go out to play?' and she said 'Yes' and got me ready.

The itchy wool tickled my face, woopsydaisy over my ears. I

snooked up a big noseful of sheepy smell. My jumper scraped down my cheeks, then my whole head burst through with a plop. It was then that Mummy said, 'When the postman comes, go with him,' and her face went blurry like in my snap of her. Daddy had let me take a photo without helping.

Then she carried on, tucking my hands in the armholes; pulling my arms through the knitted tubes like the ends of my skipping rope. We pulled down the daisy so it was all over my front – and some yellow from my egg, too. I stood there feeling thick and heavy waiting for her to say ready.

'Ready,' she said, and I skipped down the hall. All by my myself I stuck my crumply socks into my red wellies and the wind took the door out of my hand with a bang – 'No need for that racket!' – and I flew out into our yard and jumped over the gusts of wind. Every jump, I was in the air for about ten minutes.

Then Mummy came out with an apple for my pony. By then I'd worked it out. She was going to be so busy tidying things up from the wind today that I'd have to go with the postman for my dinner. As I was skipping away to the stable with the apple, I heard the cranking metal of the barn door.

Today it's windy again when I get up. My wellies are all fumbled up in the sheets. There's grass and mud in my bed, but no one will see. I clippety-clop down the stairs in my wellies, pulling my daisy jumper down as far as my knees. There's a long drib-ble of muesli from yesterday where it fell off the table, accidentally, all the way down from the daisy to the bottom of my kilt. But no one will see. Clippety-clop on the kitchen linoleum, clop-clop in the puddle of milk.

I stand on the chair to reach the cornflakes today. Out of the window the only living thing I can see is the wind, dragging across the fields like a comb through my hair. The muesli bowl's upside down under the table. I pick it up and fill it with cornflakes. They stick to my sleeve when I push my arm into the box, and come spraying out all over the place. Never mind. In the fridge there's another bottle of milk. Yesterday's has gone smelly on the table. I take the milk out of the fridge, stick my thumb through the silver top and poke my tongue in as far as I can to get the creamy bit. Yuk! It's gone cheesy. Yuk! I wipe off my tongue on the tablecloth. It's like holding a worm while wearing my mittens. I just eat raw cornflakes for a bit, pretending they're dolls' potato crisps.

Then I hear my pony in the distance. Yey! I gallop off down the hall, bang open the door saying 'No need for that racket' and run into the wind in the yard. I clop-clop in my too-big wellies across the cobbles to where the whinnying is.

Over there at the other side, the up-and-over door of the barn is rattling like thunder in the wind. I'm scared of the dark gap along the bottom of the door where it hasn't been pulled right down. Of the black strip that was big enough to put my head in to have a look.

A clump of horsehair flurries over my head from the stable door that's blown open on top. That's what it's like when there's wind. It's exciting. My fingers tug at the high-up bolt. It nips me like a bully as it clunks back in the slot.

My pony. It's as warm as sunshine in the stable and my pony's waiting for me. I push her nose away playfully and grab her shaggy mane in my fists and tug each side. I'm only teasing. 'You put your hay all over my jumper yesterday, you naughty thing. I was prickly all night.' There are gold pins all over my jumper, red prick marks all across my tummy. But she didn't do it on purpose.

We talk, me and my pony, every day. Every day in the long holidays anyway, when nobody ever comes by and Mummy is in the window watching the wheat grow. I've got to tell my pony the good idea I had in my sleep; get her on my side. I say: 'Last night I dreamed of an adventure that we can do!' My pony gives me her normal look, which is really sad, and says 'It's too dangerous.' So gloomy, like that. She tosses her head to pull her mane out of my fingers. She can be a bit rough. Mummy would say don't be petulant. I tell her off – 'Don't be so unfriendly.'

She's very nice and kind, really, is my pony; she only pretends to be upset with me sometimes, so now she says 'Sorry.' She's sorry about my prickles, and pulling her mane away, and about Mummy.

'That's OK,' I say. Funny, because *she's* the one with the sad face, so why is she saying sorry to *me*? I say 'I want you to be happy. Take off your sad face. Now, if I tell you something, you have to be excited, OK?'

I know it's hard for any pony to smile, let alone a pony with such very sad eyes as my pony. But I do want her to smile this time, so that I know she's excited about our adventure. I don't tell her that I'm too scared to do it if she won't.

'Are you my best friend in the world?' I press down on her nose and she nods into my hand. I hear her say, 'Yes, yes! Just tell me.'

'Well' – and a memory warms me all the way through like hot milk with honey: the knobble of his knee through his trousers when I lean my face against his leg; the rough smoky cloth on my face – 'We're going to stay with Daddy!'

My pony is so gloomy. She immediately points out the basic problem: we don't know where Daddy lives. You can't set off to someone's house without knowing where it is.

I've tried asking Mummy sometimes. About Daddy. All kinds of things about Daddy; where he's gone to, for example. Whether he'll come for my birthday. Why he hasn't come to mend the barn roof that's blown off. She's always been too busy stirring the soup or watching the fields to answer. 'Go and play!' she snaps. One time I ran outside when she said that, and fell over when I was practising jumping over the wind, and started crying because there was blood on my knee. When I went in again, she had started crying too. She must have seen me from the window. I stopped crying then and smiled, showing her that it didn't really hurt at all, so she could stop too. Only she didn't.

Is today the day after the day after the day after? I've woken up with even more prickles – from my home-made bed in the stable. Yesterday, before it got dark, I brought my duvet out. It's so puffy that I can't hold it all up – so it got a bit dirty in the yard. My pony just looked at me.

'I don't want to be alone in my bedroom because of the dark gap below the barn door,' I explained. Was it the day before the day before yesterday now, or the day before that, when I went to look for Mummy in the barn?

The trouble was, the postman didn't come that day. So when I got hungry I went to the barn. The door had been pulled nearly all the way down but it sticks at the bottom.

'Mummy!' I yelled, and threw myself against the door to make a thundery noise like a gong. I felt the great sheet of metal all quivery where I landed. I did that lots, until she should have called out 'No need for that racket' and come outside. She should have come out and said, 'Well, we'll just have gypsy toast again for dinner. There's nothing else in.'

But she didn't come out.

The gap was too small to wriggle under but if I lay down on my side in the dusty yard my head might just . . . if I put it sideways . . .

It was dim in there. A daddy-long-legs was strutting towards my face out of the darkness. I blew as hard as I could and it puffed away along the concrete. Far inside I could see the bottoms of the tractor's wheels. There were oil spots, a machine smell, and clumps of hay wafting on the floor. But close to me, when I moved my head a bit, there was something surprising. It was Mummy's slippers, dangling with their toes pointing in like my Ragamuffin doll. So strange because they weren't standing on anything. I reached my arm in, waved it about below them. There wasn't even anything magic, invisible. There was only air.

My pony is tossing her head where I'm squeezing her tightly round the neck, pushing my face into her scruffy mane. 'Too hard,' she says gently, but I don't want to let go. On the other hand, we both need breakfast and we've got to be sensible. I pick up a handful of her motley-coloured feed and wonder what it tastes like with milk and sugar. I had hoped for another dream last night to help with this problem of how to find Daddy. My pony says, 'Your eyes look as sad as mine today.' I nearly start to cry but my tummy's rumbling so much that I decide to go and fetch my bowl and spoon and some milk and sugar for the feed.

When I push open the stable door there is no wind at all. The sky is bright blue and full of sunshine. I do funny rubbery skips across the cobbles in my wellies without looking sideways and rush into the house to have a wee.

The kitchen doesn't look like our kitchen any more because

there's mess everywhere. I'm pulling up my pants and wandering about looking for my cereal bowl when I hear the postman's Land Rover. And I remember there's only cheesy milk.

The postman has walked in through the open door, talking in a loud breezy voice, holding out a pen and a card. He stops at the kitchen door with a funny look on his face. I give my rumply daisy jumper a quick rub, dusting off some of the dried muesli from my chest. I feel a bit naughty, noticing I'm shuffling in squelchy stuff on the floor from yesterday's dinner. The postman says, 'Where's your mother? She needs to sign for this.'

There's a brown envelope in his hand. He goes to let it drop on to the table but stops because of the spilt milk. I'm suddenly trembling with the suspense because this is it; it has to be it.

'Who's it from?' I ask. I'm nearly bursting.

'That I don't know, love. Postmark Southampton.'

Southampton!

The postman is looking at me in a daddyish way. It passes through my mind to go with him after all, but I'm sure he wouldn't let my pony come.

'Where's your mum, love?' he says kindly. He bends right down, pulls up my tights properly and pulls my kilt down on top, then he pats my arm softly. His eyes are brown and warm, almost like my pony's.

'She went to the barn,' I say, and skip past him down the hall, across the sunny cobbles and into the stable with the important information. My pony stamps her feet a bit when I rush in with the news, because she hasn't finished her breakfast. 'You old roly-poly,' I tease her. 'Daddy will give us breakfast when we get there! Come on!' I put on my riding hat and look at all the tackle hanging on the wall. It's too heavy for me.

'We won't bother with all that,' I say. I'm good at balancing on my pony's warm, bare back anyway. I climb up the side of the stall and straddle her, and dig my fingers deep into her mane.

'Southampton,' I say, kicking my heels in her belly till she decides to move. She always sees the gloomy side, my pony.

'We'll ask people along the way,' I reassure her.

We bounce across the cobbles, clippety-clop, past the jolly red Land Rover and through the open gate. I can see the postman with his jacket off, getting ready to give a great heave to the up-and-over door. Then we're away down the track in the sunshine. From my pony's back I can see the tops of the wheat nodding hello to us over the hedgerows.

ROS BARBER

Contract

I wonder about the price of things.
You fill me in.

Two hundred quid to have my legs
shattered like eggs

with a crowbar, a mere fifty more
to break my jaw and score

a general kicking. A pony sees
me pushing up daisies:

add thirty per cent
to make it look like an accident.

Two grand
to remove fingerprints from the hand

and make me untraceable –
better still

double it
and give my head a separate

burial. You can take me apart
by proxy; limb from liver from heart

that never loved you enough.
Perhaps, they can shove it

into a shoe-box.
Bring the damn thing back to you.

Dream at the Lost & Found

They gave me a ticket.
It said 'Collect'.
I went to the booth
and they brought out,
box by box,
everything I've ever lost.

An umbrella, some keys, one shoe, a Filofax.
My virginity, which I didn't want back.
My pre-pubescent crush on Doug McClure.
Thirty pounds in a purse stolen on Brighton shore.
A photo of my brother who died, gone with the purse.
My brother himself.
Rings, bracelets, knickers (don't ask),
my innocence, a library card.
A paua-shell compact from one of my aunts.
Face, more than once.
Hope, now and then.
A wedding hat, a penfriend and a silver pen.
Love in its many forms: my dad from 1972,
the first boy to chuck me, and finally, you.

Lone parent family breakfast

'You move like that,' he says, his six-year-old
fingers hopping like a thrush across the
tablecloth, 'and you get a king.'

I'm distracted; his younger brother is digging
fingers to the bottom of the Frosties
packet, mining for the pencil topper.

'Mum, you get a king!' says the eldest,
and grabs my wrists, urgently. 'I'm
only asking for a prince,' I say, obliquely.

'No,' he frowns, 'you don't get a prince.'
'I know, I know.' Pulling out the earring
that has snagged and formed a scab.

The Frosties pack is upended now,
seven-hundred and fifty grams of sugary
flakes over the table, chair and floor.

Really annoyed now, eldest son
punches me in the shoulder. 'Mum,
what is it!' 'It's nothing,' I say.

'No, what is it where you move like this'
(his fingers hop across again)
'and you get a king?'

'Draughts!' I say. 'Draughts.' He smiles,
delighted. 'You can play draughts?' He nods.
'When did you learn to play draughts?'

The day we meet again

You will be helping your wife out of a small canoe
and brushing a feather of hair out of her eyes.
It will be the morning I have finally made up my mind
to give up the foundation. The lipstick and eye-shadow

also. It will be the first hour after a long night, the first
hangover for a year or two. The first time I've ever
worn glasses instead of contacts, the first time my
leg has been cast, the third trimester of a hang-dog

pregnancy. And you –

You will be perfect. You will be just the same:
to the inch, to the ounce, to the day. I will be grey,
and you will hardly recognise me for the woman
who mystified your friends. I was, am, the storm

where your rest ends. Your lover, sworn. But the soul
of discretion, as ever. You will fleetingly find in my eyes
a familiar inflection. You will tuck your life tighter under
your arm, walk the both of you, faster, in the other direction.

Fruits of the dead

'Once before you were born, when I was five or six months preg-
nant, I spent an afternoon in a cemetery.' Her son, just turned
four, liked nothing better than to hear a story that involved him-
self, his younger self. 'Tell me about when I had a fever,' he'd
said just the other day. 'how my teacher called you and you got
a phone call in your class . . .' She'd told him that story many
times – it all became a story – how she had to leave her stu-
dents in the middle of a lecture to pick him up and take him to
the doctor. He'd been miserable, had thrown a tantrum in the
car; she'd barely been able to get him out of the car and into the
doctor's (and then everyone staring at them in the waiting room,
as if no one else had a child who'd ever misbehaved publicly).

'This was a cemetery in London, a city far away . . .' She sud-
denly couldn't remember what had brought her there – and
without her husband? She remembered that she'd been walk-
ing, walking and walking; she'd worn the wrong shoes, sandals
that her heels kept slipping out of. At last she'd found the

graveyard – had she been looking for it all along? Had that been her destination, the purpose behind all that walking? She couldn't remember. What she did remember were the berries: big thick juicy blackberries, plumper and tastier than any she'd ever eaten. Purple juice stained her hands, and still she couldn't stop picking them, devouring them by the handful. She'd felt so hungry, she couldn't get enough of them, though all the while she was thinking, these are only so plump and tasty because they're growing out of the rotting dead. It seemed wrong, not healthy, to be feeding her unborn child – so greedily – the fruits of dead people. Though she did not stop herself.

Her legs had hurt, her feet and legs were swollen, and the urge to lie down on top of one of the tombstones, granite warmed by the sun, and close her eyes, almost overwhelmed her. The other visitors – stray couples and families – kept her from giving in. She noticed that one family, Iranian maybe (why did she think that?), had brought buckets with them. They were blackberry-picking in the cemetery . . . And she'd been furtive, stealing berries by the handful, eating them as she walked where no one would see her, holding back, pretending to study a gravestone, when really it was the blackberry bush bending over it that interested her. Yet this family made no attempt to hide the purpose of their outing. Still, she felt odd, not right, though she did not stop herself. 'And now do I like berries?'

'You like them a lot. Remember in the summertime we go across the road to find them in the woods?'

'Yes, and we bring a cup to put them in . . .'

But they were straggly and few. Often sour, picked before they were ready, and never profuse. Not lush like those in London, but she and her son picked them anyway, because scavenging for food gave them something to do.

'Mom, you know what?'

'What?' she asked her son, her mind distracted, lingering still among gravestones.

'You forgot something.'

'What? What did I forget?' she asked, looking at him now, her eyes searching his as they sat next to one another on the living-room couch.

'You forgot to tell me about the cats.'

'Oh . . .' she said, 'you're right – I did.'

And so she had. One story always followed the other; that is how she had told it the first time, so that was how she must tell it again.

'Well,' she said, 'let me see . . . The cats came much later, you know, it was just last year . . . suddenly we had so many, a whole family . . .'

First, a pregnant cat had found them – no, she wasn't pregnant, she'd just given birth, and was on the search for food. She'd been left behind; they'd found her nest with five kittens in the ransacked trailer down the road. They'd taken all six cats in, hoping to find homes for them.

'And what about Bones? You forgot Bones, Mom . . .'

'Oh yes, Bones . . .' she said, more to herself than him. 'Well, one day, not long after we found the kittens, a hungry black cat just showed up, out of nowhere . . .' A cat they'd never once seen before, just black fur stretched over bones, so skinny you could see his every rib. They fed him and he longed to be taken into their home, petted and cuddled, but she didn't want him. She was constantly thrusting him out (he slunk in as she held the door open for her son), but he was so persistent, tenacious: crying at the door, then hanging by his claws on the screen window as they ate their breakfast – as if in someone's nightmare – that it seemed cruel not to give in. But she was resolved: he would live in the garage until they found a home for him. He soon grew to a normal size, his black fur thick and shiny again, but she could never get rid of that other image of him, wasted and starving, crying at the door and hanging at the window . . .

They had tried to get rid of all of them, and had found homes for two kittens, but the others . . . no one wanted them, no one at all; not even the animal shelter would take them. The shelter had so many different stories: 'There's an infectious disease going around right now . . .' 'There's been a fire in the basement . . .' 'Our cats are in quarantine . . .' 'We have a moratorium on cats right now . . .' 'Quarantine', 'moratorium': she was sure they just threw around those terms to scare away callers.

Once she saw a notice in the papers about a black cat that had disappeared; the couple was 'desperately searching'. Suddenly hopeful, she'd called them. On the phone she saw that Bones didn't quite fit the description (no patch of white fur under his chin), but she sensed the couple's eagerness to believe otherwise, and invited them over to see him. For once Bones sat in their living room, licking and preening himself in a cushioned chair, looking as if he'd always belonged there.

Despite his inattention to them, his smaller size and lack of a white patch, the couple almost convinced themselves that Bones was their Blackie. She found herself encouraging them, and when this didn't work (they suddenly emerged, as if from a dream, to announce, 'No, it isn't him'), 'Well, why don't you take him anyway? He's friendly and neutered, I'm afraid you'll never find your Blackie . . .' But they left empty-handed.

And then the mama cat got pregnant again. Looking at the cat's swollen belly made her feel ill. Any day there would be even more cats to contend with. 'You have to do something,' she told her husband. 'I don't care what it is . . .'

He made an appointment with the veterinarian. He never described the procedure, only that he'd walked into an office with an armful of live cats, then walked out with two cardboard carrying cases, very heavy ones. There were people in the waiting room – he'd wondered what they were thinking.

'And then Daddy buried them . . .'

'Yes, he took them to the woods.' He hadn't described that part to her either, hadn't wanted to. It was something he'd done for her. He'd carried the cardboard cases and a shovel across the road. In a secluded spot in the woods, one not visible from the road, he'd dug a wide hole, then dumped the contents of the two cases in. The bodies fell one on top of the other; the last was Bones, now a good solid weight, his shiny black fur covering up the smaller bodies. Digging farther in the woods, he'd found more dirt and leaves to bury them with. Deep enough, he'd thought. But walking through the path in the woods some weeks later, they'd noticed vultures. What could those birds be after? Without thinking, they'd gone over to investigate. She hadn't wanted her son to see, to know, but it was too late: the giant birds were chewing on small bones.

'What are all those bones? Where did all those bones come from?' their son had asked, and she and her husband exchanged glances. You deal with this one, her husband's look said: this is your doing. And so she told her son the story because that is what she'd always done.

'Mom,' her son said, nudging her again. 'Let's go look for berries now.'

'Yes, we'll go,' she answered, though it wasn't time – too soon, the sun too faint. The fruits would be only green and bitter versions of themselves, she knew.

LYNN WALTON

Left behind

This is how he feels   Sour cream trespassing in
                                her morning coffee.

This is how he walks   Drowsy fingers in
                                melting butter.

This is how he sounds   A chandelier
                                plunging on stones.

This is how he touches   Eavesdropping fingers
                                on her vibrant hands.

This is how he grows   Forgotten bonsai on an
                                undusted window ledge.

This is how he talks   Past tense.

This is how he cries   Camouflage.

Shuts my eyes whilst I run
Plunging disappointment
Of a prince's hoof
I listen for the intrusion
That chant as I pass
Of gnarled molten shapes
Pours its muted outflow
The thirteenth stair
Place each foot
Exactly where I
Seeps its uncompromising way
A crackling thicket
Woven into straw
Its strands have been
Gropes at the dusky window
The sun feebly
With fetid breath
That prowls
In cunning cloudswirl
Its top is lost
And blackthorn tendrils
From fairytale towers
Spawned itself
This staircase has

Child's journey to bed

(read from bottom to top)

Cinderella married a foot fetishist

You can't remember the shape of my face
the feel of my dress, the curve of my thigh.

You spent the night with your eyes licking my feet
seduced by my naked, clinging shoes.

When we were fused, I was the envy of my friends
but you'd gift-wrapped the truth in a Barbie wedding.

Now you paint my toenails opinionless pink
buy me matching lipstick and hope the words seep out the
same.

You cream the soles of my feet with rose-scented obsession
and make me dance barefoot on your intermittent spine.

But remember that these are devoted social climbing feet –
and they don't make Dr Martens in glass.

Vulnerable adults

When the pamphlet came through the mail-slot they were in the middle of a small fight. A small fight being when they teased each other, but with higher than normal voices and more rigid than usual faces. It could have turned into a big fight: things were getting higher and stiffer by the minute, but the pamphlet stopped all that.

WANTED: GOOD HOMES FOR VULNERABLE ADULTS

'Give me that,' said Lauren. The pamphlet said that the social services were desperate to find good homes where vulnerable adults could re-integrate themselves back into the community.

'Pretty good money,' said Jacko, leaning over Lauren's shoulder. She frowned.

'This is crazy – anybody could get hold of this.'

'They're retards, aren't they?'

'What do you mean, retards?'

'Vulnerable adults. They're mongoloids, aren't they?'

'Who, the social services?' She laughed at her joke.

'Let's get some! We could train them to clean. We could get them to build a shed, and then they could sleep in it.'

'I could train one to be my personal maid.'

'She could iron your shoulder pads.'

'Don't be gross, Jacko. Shoulder pads went out years ago.'

They both laughed.

'God,' said Lauren. 'I can't believe we said what we just said.'

Jacko took the pamphlet and put it in his 'miscellaneous' folder.

Tonight, Lauren was going Chinese. There was something so elegant about slicing vegetables with a diagonal slant. The way you sliced vegetables was important. She arranged the vegetables on the cutting board in a nice pattern: green against red and orange. The radio played some soothing oriental-style music. Then Jacko came in from the living room where he was watching television.

'I can't believe she's really having an affair with him. He's the next door neighbour.'

'Who's the next door neighbour?'

'They only just got married!'

'What are you talking about?'

– but Jacko had gone back into the living room.

Lauren sat down at the table and tried to concentrate on the new candelabra she'd just bought. The kitchen was full of shadows, warm light from the candles, cold light from the blue gas ring. She heated the wok until it smoked and spat at her when she tossed the pretty vegetables in. The soothing music had changed. They were playing some weird opera stuff with lots of heavy cymbals. She switched the radio off and listened to the soft boom of advertisements from the television in the other room.

Later, when she lay in bed next to Jacko, she tossed and turned and finally switched the bedside light back on and picked up her magazine. There was an article about something called feng shui. It was all about how to decorate your home to keep the evil spirits out. At least, that's what she thought it was about. It was hard to understand all the diagrams. How could a pine tree be a poison arrow? She threw the magazine down.

'I can't breathe,' she said.

Jacko was asleep. She touched his hair.

Jacko was making puppets. Their little hands and feet were lined up in a row. When he made their faces, he couldn't decide whether to make them happy or sad. Finally, he decided to make them look blank. It was up to him, he thought, to make them seem happy or tragic.

'What are you doing?' said Lauren.

'What does it look like I'm doing?' said Jacko.

Lauren shrugged and went into the other room. She made herself a cup of tea, and then felt bad and made one for Jacko too. Moody. She stood by the window that looked out on to the back gardens of their row of terraced houses. She saw, in the garden two houses down, a small girl sitting on an ornamental bench by two gnomes and a little blue plastic pond. Her hands were folded together, and the corners of her mouth were turned down. She was wearing a large red corduroy dress and a red jacket. Beneath the jacket's hood, two slightly slanted eyes stared into the pond.

'Jacko!' cried Lauren.

'Lauren!' cried Jacko. He came in from the other room, his hands covered in glue.

'The neighbours have got a vulnerable adult.' She pointed at the girl and stared, the tea-steam rising into her face. 'She looks so *unhappy*.'

Jacko put his arm around Lauren and squeezed her. 'Darling,' he said. 'Let's you and I go somewhere together – deep into a forest or by the wild seashore. Just you and I – away from all this misery.' He waved his hand at the back yards.

'Please, Jacko. I'm so tired.' She turned from the window and walked out of the room.

'You're just projecting, Lauren,' said Jacko.

Later on, after he'd put the finishing touches to the puppets, he climbed up to the bedroom and watched her sleeping in the dark. He switched on the bedside lamp and she moved. He leaned over her and saw the fine web of wrinkles just coming under her eyes. She looked like an angel with her mouth wide open like that. He kissed her face. She didn't wake up.

Jacko watched the television. It was an American horror movie. Aliens were penetrating the human mind and turning them into inter-galactic slaves. The male aliens had pointed beards and V-shaped bodies with long capes. Jacko wore his puppets on either hand like gloves. On the screen, some aliens in miniskirts were seducing handsome men and then frying their heads. Bleep, bleep went the inbuilt phaser guns as their bursts of red light bore into the eyes of the victims. The sky turned violet as the aliens took over the world and unusual plants blossomed on the hard shoulders of the interstate.

'What a load of shit,' said Lauren, who'd come up behind him.

Lauren lay on the floor with her eyes shut. The radio was playing something Indian-sounding. She tried to imagine she was in a field. The grass swayed. The sun pulsed above the distant mountain range. The sound of insects rose above the tinny music, or maybe it was just the radio hissing. Then the image receded. She felt the painted floorboards creak under her back as the footsteps came towards her.

'I'd like to interrupt this programme with a message from the social services.'

Lauren opened her eyes.

'I'd like to interrupt this programme with a message from the social services.' Jacko leaned over her with his two puppets on either hand.

'Daddy made me do this and it really hurt,' said the puppet. 'Show us what Daddy made you do,' said Jacko. He pushed the puppets together and made a slurping noise.

Lauren shut her eyes.

'Ha, ha,' she said. 'Very funny.'

Lauren and her friend were sitting in the kitchen drinking ginger tea and talking and eating sun-dried bananas from Guatemala.

'I'm a sucker for details,' said Lauren's friend. 'Sometimes I watch a film just for the scenery and to see what people are wearing.'

Lauren poured some more tea.

'Even if it's a really stupid film – or one of those Jackie Collins things.'

'Oh yeah,' said Lauren. 'Bonkbusters!'

They laughed.

Lauren leaned over the table. 'Don't you ever wish you were just a character in a book and not the person reading it?'

Lauren's friend frowned. 'Kind of. But you can pretend. I mean, I think you're supposed to.'

'You could pretend that you're a character in a different novel reading a novel.'

'But that's really *passé*, isn't it? And anyway, you end up feeling just as self-conscious as before. I mean, the idea is not to be self-conscious, isn't it?'

Lauren nodded. 'You're right. The best thing is just not to think about things too much.'

'I *think* I know what you mean.'

They both laughed and ate some more bananas.

Jacko came into the kitchen. He had his arm high up in the air with one of his hand-puppets on. 'I'd like to interrupt this programme with another message from the social services.'

Lauren put her hands over her eyes because she knew what was going to happen.

Jacko lowered the puppet to shoulder height, and curled his hand to make the puppet look tired and unhappy. Its head tilted to one side. 'Mommy bit me,' said the puppet.

There was a long silence as they all stared at the puppet. Then Lauren's friend laughed really loudly. 'God that's so funny. Jacko, you are such a *scream*.' She went up to the puppet and snatched it from his hand. 'Did you make this yourself? Look at the stitching!' She examined the puppet and turned it inside out.

Jacko smiled and took the puppet back.

'Do you mind,' said Lauren, her forehead creased with frowns. 'We haven't seen each other for ages.'

Jacko poured himself some tea and left the kitchen. Lauren sat with her friend, but suddenly she felt like there wasn't very much left to say. It was getting dark so quickly in the afternoons.

'Oh I get it,' said Lauren's friend suddenly. 'It's like those dolls they use in the police.'

Lauren and Jacko stood in the kitchen and shouted at each other.

'You were trying to *undermine* me in front of your friend,' said Jacko.

'You were trying to get all the attention,' said Lauren. She wanted to say something else too.

'No I wasn't.'

'Yes you were.'

'No I was. Yes I were.' Jacko danced around the room.

'Shut up!' said Lauren. She tried to grab Jacko by the waist so she could hit him. He danced away from her. She lunged at him and they started kissing, tumbling into the stairwell that was painted lemon-yellow like the ones in the breakfast cereal ads. 'I hate you,' said Lauren.

'I've heard that somewhere before,' said Jacko.

Lauren was watching the vulnerable adult again. She was always there. She sat very still, staring straight ahead. The girl was wearing the same dress and coat, and she always had the same expression on her face, staring into the ugly fish pond that didn't look like it had any fish in it, next to the two gnomes painted yellow and red and blue.

It was really so cold outside now, and Lauren couldn't

understand how the girl didn't notice. She shivered and switched
the little table lamp on. It made the sky look black. 'I don't know.
She seems quite peaceful out there. Kind of serene.'

'They say they're really horny.'

'What?'

'They say they're really active, sexually. They fuck each other
all the time. In the homes.'

Lauren looked out at the girl.

'She's probably on the pill. Bet she's thinking about her
boyfriend back in the home.'

'That's not fair!' said Lauren. 'They bring them out here and
just let them get all lonely!'

'Yeah,' said Jacko. 'It's called re-integrating them into the
community. Not everyone in the community is lonely. I'm not
lonely, am I?' Jacko came up behind Lauren and put his arms
around her waist. He kissed her neck and made all the fine
hairs stand up. He slipped his hand up her skirt, and she
turned to kiss him.

'You're a pervert,' she said.

'So are you,' he said.

She reached behind her and pulled down the blind.

Jacko watched the television with the sound turned down. He
liked watching the facial expressions of the actors without
knowing what they were saying. Sometimes he liked to imagine
what they might say in Jacko's world.

Lauren was trying to talk to him. 'I'm looking at everyone
and wondering if they might be vulnerable adults now.'

'I guess it is a pretty bad neighbourhood.'

'Ha ha. I'm serious.'

'No, I*'m* serious.'

'Do you think we should move?'

He could hear her behind him, trying to assemble her new aromatherapy steamer. He watched the face of an actor, who was standing in a swanky-looking room with another actor. They were probably talking about how much they really liked to be actors and what a great job they had.

'It's not the fact that there are vulnerable adults around,' said Lauren. 'It's the idea that most of the people around here look like they might be retarded.'

The steamer fell apart again.

'Fuck,' said Lauren.

'Try reading the instruction manual.'

'Leave me alone.'

'Feeling pre-menstrual, darling? Let me make the dinner, do the dishes, wash the stinking cat bowl. Polish the dildo.' Jacko jumped up from his chair and switched the television off.

Lauren screamed and threw her cushion at him.

'Lick the pan,' said Jacko. 'Bake the hamster. Walk the dog. Build the shed.'

She ran out of the living room and went upstairs.

Jacko switched the television back on, this time with the sound up.

Lauren lay down on the bed in the guest room, where it was always chilly from the heating never being switched on. She lay there without moving for twenty minutes, getting colder and colder and more rigid. Then she heard the sound of cutlery like it was coming from far away. Then the pots and pans and the smell of food. She was almost too cold to get up and wrap herself in the woollen blanket by the window and make herself warm.

'I'm not going to look out there,' said Lauren to herself. But she saw the red jacket from the corner of her eye.

She curled up on the bed until Jacko came upstairs and told her dinner was ready, and that she would suffer in her next life for the good things that he did for her and the bad things she did to him.

'I've got *scars*,' he said.

'I just want some peace and quiet,' she said. She couldn't believe that she was crying.

'I think they took you for a ride with that steamer,' said Jacko.

Lauren showed Jacko the pamphlet. 'I think we should do it.'

Jacko gave her back the pamphlet.

'I think it would be really cleansing. It says here that it's good for your body and your mind. And you can reach the highest spiritual plane if you practise it a lot.'

'We could get a black belt in meditation,' said Jacko.

Lauren threw the pamphlet down on the table.

'It's better than hanging around the house all day playing with puppets and watching television.'

'Have you been playing with my puppets when I haven't been looking?'

'It's only two hours a week. I've got to find some kind of way out of this mess. I want to start feeling relaxed. Happy. You know, important stuff like that. There's no point me doing it if you're going to be crazy all over the house and drive me nuts with you.'

Jacko's long face got longer. 'I'm not going to some gym to sit with a bunch of social worker types searching for inner harmony. Call me old-fashioned.'

'Maybe you're right.' Lauren sighed. When she left the kitchen, Jacko took the pamphlet and put it in his 'miscellaneous' folder.

*

Lauren and Jacko curled up under the duvet together. There was no noise, and the skylight framed a perfect square of stars.

'Do you ever wish you believed in God?' said Lauren.

Jacko twitched. He was dreaming.

When Lauren got home from shopping the house was very quiet. She spread her new things out on the table. Sandalwood incense. Camomile bubble bath. A book of *Illustrated Bible Stories*. Why not? The stories looked nice, and she remembered some of them from her childhood. Joseph and the Many-Coloured Coat, for example. The pictures were like children's pictures: that primitive blue, pink, yellow combination and lots of lambs and fluffy animals. In fact, it *was* a children's book. Where was Jacko? She went into the living room but he wasn't there. The puppets were gone. She ran up the stairs but the bedrooms were empty. She moved towards the window. 'I'm not going to look,' she said.

MELANIE GILES

Stonework

For my twin

You will try the words in your mouth,
mineral of mica and glauconite,
the gloss of flint in bone-white chalk,
scrapbooks of stone like porous skin
     in which you note
the feel of greensand, soft and dank as moss,
the secret ferrous nodule, puckered in a fault.

I weigh stone's worth against the eye,
stratigraphy of stream and bedding plane,
the ashlar's chisel cut and mortared line,
how sandstone rots, how shales will split
like books left open in the rain:
how chalk will flake and weather, leaving
on our hands the milky taste of loam.

Digging, we learn a geological tongue;
how bedrock sounds to the blade,
the hollow tap of lime and rip of clay,
the weather-crumbled sands of millstone grit.
Grazed hands give back the scent of earth
      on warm, raw palms, sweat-stung,
dampened with milt and rain.

We each become attendant to our skin,
the curve of rib, the scoured wrist and limb,
lather of dust and salt, and sudden warmth
of muscles pliant as silt under the palm.
Like a moment from childhood, fists curled tight
and sleeping back-to-back,
      like ammonites.

Weaverthorpe

Aerial photography has revealed the presence of a group
of crescent shaped enclosures along a raised lobe of land
in the Great Wolds Valley, East Yorkshire. These are con-
nected to trackways which run down to the seasonal
stream in the base of the valley, the Gypsy Race. They
suggest the movement of livestock between the
Weaverthorpe settlement and open land or pasture to
the south. At the juncture of these trackways and the
enclosure ditches are found clusters of square barrow
burials, typical of the later Iron Age of this area.

(paraphrased from Cathy Stoertz
Ancient Landscapes of the Yorkshire Wolds, 1997)

they know the rites of way:
my hand has only to flick
the swaying, high-boned hip,
to nudge the pendulous head,
set udders swinging between
hind legs patched with soil and shit.

by them I am known,
my herder's gait.
their names are my lineage,
their smell, warm turf,
sweat and hair-grease,
grass with the scent of cream to it,
rich on the lip,
          a bellyful.

each jaw longer than my handspan,
there is no tongue thicker
its curl   crop   rip.
I know too, the carving of breast from bone,
how each death holds the slather of birth.
the warm peel of hide and flesh, the blood
                            a pulse,
rich and sticky, seeping into soil.
watering it,
        like the stream in flood
guzzles at gravel.
this surge is in every vein,
throbbing in the neck,
in the sweat and heft of ribs
and flank.
        the gape
of each body in spate,
rhythms of thigh and hip
and thirst.

we are made
through this slow stumble
and trip of hooves and feet.
the herd's rise and dip
where we have worn the earth's skin
        into scars.

so we mark the land's curve
with our dead, cut them into its bone.
they watch us come
and go.
our crossing of the land by their marks,
      watering at dawn
      the noonday graze
      the herding home.

we are their thread, living and dead
woven each day
through our warp
      and weft.

Physalis

all day I have thirsted for you.
filled my pockets with mandarins
round and hard as your heel.

a spill of peel
    and juice, the ochred zest,
a greediness of flesh
    unquenched.

the delicate tracery of pith
a fretwork,
    like the veins in your wrist,
where tongue and spine seem
to connect.

as *Physalis'* fragile cage of skin
encase what is desired
    in moth-wing skeins,
the hidden fruit, shadow of berry
    and flame.

S w i m m i n g   w i t h   m y   t w i n

Front crawl. You're off
in the amniotic rush
of water and air, greedy for it,
slicing through, the muscle gleaming
on the turn, the crook
of your arm
          carving
past your head. Pushing
off,
          with the flick of a foot
into the raw gape
of water and light.

As you pass, I dip
in the steady pulse of breaststroke,
symmetry of ankle and palm,
in which I hear my heartbeat,
slower than yours,
learning the rise and fall of it,
          surprised
by the claustrophobic silence,
lapping in my ears.

Adrift
    and longing
for the nestled curve of your body with mine,
the way we might have touched,
to be sure of each other's presence.
    I kick free
make for the wash of water
in your wake,
the graze of light.

Anna Black

Tick Tock

She was thin; so thin that when she hugged her arms close you could see the sharp bone of her shoulder cut through the skin. She shivered despite the late summer sun. Her feet had been pushed into pink strappy sandals. Her cracked heels overhung the backs by a good inch. I remember thinking that the wooden sole must dig into her flesh when she walked. Her hair was wild; a black, uncombed riot. She had one of those brightly coloured children's barrettes vainly trying to keep it in check. It was a Teletubby – the red one – Dipsy? God knows. Anyway, it didn't work.

Her face was geisha white, her cheeks mapped with the palest blue veins and her eyes huge, dark and vacant. The one thing she did passionately was smoke. She sucked on the cheap roll-up with an intensity that was frightening, ignoring the small boy at her feet. He was running up and down, glee-fully pushing a plastic tractor, bouncing over the sidewalk and crashing into the road. He was kind of cute; old enough to be interesting and to do his own toilet, but still chubbily chunky and clumsy. Alistair and I had this long-running joke about babies. 'If you want one,' I used to tell him, 'you'll have to have it. I've got better things to do. There's more to it that buying train sets at Hamley's, you know.' This kid had probably never even heard of Hamley's. Not that he looked bothered as he rode roughshod through the dog shit. His mother watched but did nothing.

As soon as she caught sight of me she became animated – rambling on with a garbled story about losing her giro and not having money to buy food.

'I've not got my handbag,' I said. That was true but my purse was lying snugly in my jacket pocket. She seemed to expect my embarrassed indifference and just gave a brief smile before moving on. I looked back and saw her accosting another smartly dressed woman returning home from work.

I couldn't forget her. I felt guilty. I even went back out into the street to look for her but she had gone. When I told Alistair he just told me not to be soft.

'She's a scrounger,' he said. 'Some scrubber living off the state, who we – you and me, darling – work long hours to support.'

Alistair always made me feel better.

It must have been a week or so later: I was already in the car waiting for Alistair who had forgotten his mobile. She can't have seen me but she rounded on him with a wide smile. The child looked as if it had been licked with a flannel but she was just as wild. Her dress was a clash of colours. It was too short and she looked like an overgrown kid playing at Mummies. It suited her.

I caught snatches of the conversation. 'No change for the gas meter – lost giro – alone – hungry.' Alistair jingled his pockets.

'That's her,' I said, once he had got in. 'She's the one I told you about.'

Alistair looked back in the rear mirror. 'Hmm. She's a pretty little thing.'

'How much did you give her?' I asked.

'Oh, not much,' he assured me. 'If you give in to them, that's it. Can't have her pestering us all the time.' He fell silent.

We stopped for petrol and he tossed me his wallet to pay. I knew he had just been to the cashpoint but there was only a tenner left. Alistair never took out less than a hundred pounds.

He didn't mention her again until after dinner. We were curled up together on the sofa when he just came out with it.

'She reminds me of you, you know – when we first met. All that youth and vitality. Challenging life.'

Charming, I thought to myself. Thanks for the compliment, fifteen years on.

It got worse.

'Don't you think there's something really – well, sexy about a young woman and a baby?'

'It's not a baby,' I said tartly, getting up. 'It's at least three years old. You've never said this was a fetish of yours.'

I think he knew then he'd upset me because he changed the subject and we never talked of it again. I remember standing in front of the mirror that night. Thrusting out my flat belly and trying to picture what I would look like pregnant. Would he think I was sexy?

I had a big case on in Brussels. There were the usual problems and I ended up staying away for a couple of weeks – well, nearer four, really. I spoke to Alistair most nights. That is, our respective answering machines talked, but that was nothing new. It was worth it. I won. We drank champagne to celebrate, and then some more back in the London office. The party carried on. I did try and call Alistair but he'd already left work and the home number was engaged.

If I hadn't been so drunk I would have been quicker on my feet. As it was I just keeled over like a yacht on high seas. I didn't realise the kid had taken my bag at first. When I did, I really didn't care.

Sod it, I thought. Let him have it. Plenty more where that came from. I still had my bottle of champagne. With no money or cards I decided to walk home through the park. You make these rash decisions when you're as high as a kite. It was a wonderful night. I kicked off my heels to dance in the dew, waving my champagne bottle to the Milky Way. I saluted the statue of Peter Pan and solemnly toasted his spirit. Yup! I'd made up my mind. I'd soon be reading tales of Captain Hook and the lost boys to my own little darlings. I couldn't wait to tell Alistair my decision. I tossed the half-full bottle to the gentleman wearing the riding hat waiting at the bus stop.

'Home, James!' I shouted. I was having a ball.

There's something voyeuristic about the night in the city. Peering through uncurtained windows at snapshots of people's lives. I revelled in it. I wanted it too. I wanted to have it all.

They made a beautiful couple. She wore a red beaded dress. Haute couture, if you don't mind. I'd bought it to celebrate my Christmas bonus. It was a sexy off-the-shoulder number. She had a small tattoo on her upper right arm. A butterfly. She tilted her head confidentially towards Alistair's, eagerly listening to what he was saying. Then she threw back her head and laughed. Her neck was long and slender and at the moment, very tempting. I had to admit she brushed up very nicely – and yes, she did look something like I once had. Or was I just kidding myself?

My feet were throbbing now. They were bruised and cut. I had spilt champagne all down my front. I was truly dishevelled. As I stood there, clutching the bars at the windows that held the double-glazed life at bay, I could have been an inmate of the old Bethlehem, screaming abuse at the well-coiffured visitors.

The child came running in. His pyjama top was tucked in and the bottoms pulled up high over his rounded tummy. He was waving a train around his head like an aeroplane. They were a picture-perfect family, perfectly horrified at the vision at their window.

I screamed. I hammered at the door. I shouted foul-mouthed obscenities that I never knew I could. No one came, except the police. Two fresh-faced boys facing a ranting she-devil who would have caused the dervishes to turn tail and run.

With my head pushed down inside the squad car, I was vaguely aware of the low-voiced conversation at the door.

'I've never seen her in my life, officer. She just appeared out of the blue, screaming like this. I wish I could help, but my son – you know – I don't want him scared like this.'

I must have looked like a cartoon loon with my mouth hanging open and gesturing wildly. I did try and explain but I couldn't prove anything, you see. I had no identification.

'You must have ID,' they said. 'Everyone has ID. How about a friend to back your story up?'

They humoured me and I did try, honest, I really did. But I couldn't think of anyone except the gentleman with the riding hat at the bus stop by Peter Pan.

'Peter Pan,' I offered, pleased as punch that I could give them something. 'Peter Pan will tell you who I am.'

I couldn't understand the way they looked at me. Out of the corner of my eye I saw one of them gesturing to the other, his finger screwing what little brains he had. I couldn't make them understand.

I have to ask to be taken to the loo and as I wash my hands I can see myself in the mirror. I am thin; so thin that when I hug my arms close to stop them trembling, my bones jut out from the threadbare robe, its flowery bloom faded grey. My hair is wild about my shoulders, knotted and matted. No one takes the time to sort it. I yank out a white hair, twirling in a curl and wrap it tight around my finger so it's a throbbing barley twist of red and white. It hurts. My face is pasty grey and I have a sore on my lip. My eyes – well, my eyes are dead. There is nothing worth seeing.

The nurse offers me a cigarette and I hang over the basin and suck at it with all the strength I have left. In the mirror, I catch her eye.

'You will ask Peter, won't you? He'll tell you who I am. He knows me,' I plead. Even to my ears I sound unconvincing.

I often think of them as I sit alone in here. I put them in different scenes – Alistair playing with a large train set while the boy looks on. Her greeting the postman with a smile as she answers the door – but my favourite is the one where she sits reading the boy a story and her wild hair is spread over him like a blanket. He howls with laughter as she does the tick-tock of Captain Hook's crocodile. I like this one and replay it over and over as I rock from side to side, crooning quietly so they can't hear me. Maybe they are all right. Maybe I am not well.

MARLYNN ROSARIO

Travelling by numbers

Poppies felt-tip the verges
keeping our East we go South,
a tractor curries the field.

This morning, her emptied room,
her screams, that fear of flying things.
I caught the creature in drained glass,
trapped it with careful card,
left it to freedom on the open sill.

Now, weighted by her nineteen years,
jigsawed by possessions, blind at the rear,
we snail the motorway umbilical.

Looking back she is all my view.
She nods in the mirror-frame,
beats time to something I cannot hear,
looks past my sly eyes to something I cannot see.
I bite my tongue on remembering.

Arriving is goodbye, I leave her,
a moth bewildered after brief entrapment.
Keeping my East, returning is already familiar.
She is South of the North of me.

Pricking the damsons

I did as I was told, despite the bitterness.
Risked waspy branches to pluck them, bellied with summer
pricked them where they pearled the trampled grass
filled the wire sieve more than once.

I followed your instructions, prepared thoroughly,
dried a thick glass jar,
wiped off bloom to an aubergine shine,
ignored blood when I pricked their whale-back skins.
How the juice bruised my fingers.
I sowed salt, measured sugar between the layers.

You recommended waiting, months, a year, longer,
promised porty sweetness, vintage memories.

How was it then, that when I checked the glass today
I found them rimed with rot, mildewed with a rank frost,
suck-cheeked and withered?

I thought I'd done everything right.
Was it a faulty seal, insistent air, careless hands?
Or something beyond our eyes, specking deep
beneath the flesh, marking the seed?

Giraffe-necked woman

Giraffe-necked women with shrunk-apple faces
stare from the covers of the *National Geographic*.
Stemmed courage glints above the weight of silk
on their embroidered shoulders.
Read their beauty like the age of a tree.

You gift me chains of silver, baby pearls.
I have swallowed all my rings,
the nurture- suffer- mother- ring.
I've lost count, they coil, snaking
the lining of my throat, I could choke.

That thing I do, moving my head as though double-jointed,
side to side to side on still shoulders,
like an extra from *The King of Siam*, it's nothing.

Look carefully, beneath the thinning skin
circles crease and pucker, my chin pouches the rim.
Didn't you guess when you called me *stiff-necked, stubborn*?
What is your weight of chains to a brass-necked woman?

Sisterly love

Jane's sister Peaches is downshifting. She's decided to go into the office less and to delegate more. She's applied to have a baby.

'What do you mean, applied?' says Jane, vigorously buttering economy white slices. (Or rather low-fat-spreading them. Jane does not buy butter. She has not the natural feline sleekness of her sister.)

'Slip of the tongue,' says Peaches. She stands in Jane's kitchen in her dark smart suit, picking into a packet of Hulahoops. 'I mean, try for.'

Freudian slip, thinks Jane, sniffing. She mashes boiled egg vigorously into mayonnaise – or rather low-fat salad cream – and calls Dario and Dimitri for their tea.

Peaches surveys her nephews tepidly. She has already decided that her baby will not be like these children. Dario is picking his nose; Dimitri lifts the top off his sandwich suspiciously and the corners of his mouth turn down. Definitely

Peaches' child will be different. She will be delightful and biddable, petite and perfectly formed – a little peach.

'Small problem,' says Jane, throwing the low-fatty knife at the sink as Dario routinely ducks.

'What's that?' pouts Peaches.

'Paternity. Unless you've opened an account at a sperm bank, you need a mate.'

'And they have to do the P-thing,' supplements Dimitri with a mouthful of sandwich.

'Go and watch *Cosby*,' instructs Jane, but Dimitri says, 'Can't. Dario's still playing Sonic the Hedgehog. And he's got the controls all eggy,' he adds. Dimitri is a rather finicky child.

'He's right, though,' says Jane when the kitchen is free of earwigging offspring. 'They do have to do the P-thing. Penetration, it's called. Another name for it is non-safe sex, so you'll need to check out all applicants.'

She sweeps the crumbs off the table to the floor and plonks down a bottle of Frascati and two glasses.

'I thought you were going out,' says Peaches.

'One for the road. You're not really babysitting here in that suit, are you, Peaches?'

Would that I were not, thinks Peaches, as sounds of sibling squabbling seep from the living room. 'It's only for an hour,' she says, shrugging. 'You said Paul's due back about seven.'

'Peaches has a problem,' Jane tells her husband later that evening. She arrived back from the PTA meeting to find Paul lounging on the floor watching *Fantasy Football* and her sister already gone. Jane has flopped into the big armchair and Paul is now fiddling absentmindedly with her appreciative toes. 'She needs a man,' Jane explains, as Paul has expressed no interest in her sister's dilemma.

'Peaches must have thousands of men. What's she done with them all, eaten them?'

'She downshifted them. She read about it in the Sunday papers.'

'Can't she get some more?' says Paul. She'd be a great catch for anyone. Nice tits.' Paul is not a new man.

'Nicer than mine?' challenges Jane, confronting him bountifully. Paul lowers his eyelids in appreciative speculation by way of reply and then turns again to the screen.

Jane looks at Paul. She watches his long lashes, his hard-boned cheek, the chinline already hazed with evening stubble. She watches the way his dark hair curls crisply into the nape of his neck.

'You're a bit of a dish, you know,' says Jane softly. Paul recognises the invitation. He pulls Jane's legs slowly towards him. Just as she is about to slide in an undignified heap on to the floor Paul catches her, pulls her legs around his waist and buries his head deep into her breasts. Paul bites gently, patiently, at the fabric of her top while Jane fumbles with fastenings and fabrics until further progress is achievable. 'Mister Ever-Ready,' whispers Jane.

A little while later Jane says, 'Poor Peaches. She'd give her eye teeth for a bit of that, you know. A gorgeous guy like you, strong and safe.'

But Jane is wrong. Not about Paul, but about her sister's base-rate bargaining. Peaches would not give her eye teeth, or any part of her groomed anatomy. What Peaches would give is a thousand pounds.

'You're joking,' says Jane numbly.

'It's a good offer,' says Peaches. Today being Saturday, she is wearing blue jeans and a T-shirt. Peaches' jeans have a Lycra element so they fondle her proportions with piquant proximity and her T-shirt is doorstep-test-fresh. Nevertheless she is, by her workday standards, casually attired. Jane wears a Garfield top and Wellington boots (she had popped out the back to feed the guinea pigs). It is not yet eleven so none of her family are fully awake. Perhaps this accounts for the sensation of surreal imbalance which Jane is currently experiencing.

'It's a very good offer,' Peaches insists again. 'You could go on holiday. Or get the car fixed.'

Jane has opened the fridge to get the milk but her fingers move magnetically to the wine bottle. She pours the dregs into a tumbler with a wavering hand, absentmindedly topping up with diet cola.

'Let me get this straight,' says Jane calmly. 'You want to hire Paul out for stud, for personal use, for one thousand pounds.'

'A one-off payment,' agrees Peaches.

'Why?'

'Obvious. He's got good physique, he's healthy, and he's quite bright.'

'Not a unique combination, however,' says Jane eventually.

'But he's here and he's available.' Her sister's wide eyes begin to narrow contentiously and Peaches hastens to clarify. 'I mean, no tedious references to chase or embarrassing interviews. And he's devoted to you and the boys, so there would be no emotional complications.'

'Peaches, that's exactly why there would be complications! What if you change your mind about wanting to go it alone —'

'I shall get an au pair, of course.'

'Don't quibble. If anything went wrong, you'd point to him.'

'My solicitor could draw up an agreement,' says Peaches. Unused to demurral at her contractual arrangements, she is beginning to sound perplexed.

'You're crazy.' Jane is flushed with exasperation and alcoholic cola. She wants to shake her sister and shout about emotional need and psychological hurt but it appears that Peaches' appraisal of her project is primarily fiscal. 'Have you never heard of the Child Support Agency?'

'My solicitor said we could get round that,' says Peaches. She perches on the work-top looking glum. Jane says more gently:

'Look Peaches, you haven't thought this through. You forget how demanding children are. Dario and Dimitri are Paul's, and you don't like them that much. I know you're going to have a beautiful little girl called Aureola or something, but they grow – they get minds of their own. And a solicitor can't alter facts. Can't you ask your solicitor to do it for you himself? He sounds a penetrating sort of bloke,' she adds as an afterthought.

'My solicitor is a woman,' Peaches objects. She gets down, looking irked. 'If I'd gone ahead and had an affair with Paul behind your back, I could have got exactly what I want for nothing. But I'm a moral person, Jane. I came to you, I made you a generous offer. Why do you have to go picking faults?'

'Do it then!' shouts Jane. 'Go ahead and seduce Paul, if you think you can. Just don't try to buy him off me.'

'I don't take, I trade,' says Peaches primly. 'I have my ethical standards.' And she flounces away.

'D'you think if you want something that's not yours, it's OK to take it as long as you pay for it?' Jane asks Paul that night. She is in the bathroom flossing and he has come in for a slash but seeing her warm and naked body he becomes distracted.

'No,' says Paul, answering her question eventually, his lips still close to her bare shoulders. 'It's called a bribe, that. But rights and wrongs are funny things. I'd kill to save you and the kids a minute of worry. Is that immoral?'

'A bit excessive, for only a minute,' concedes Jane. 'It's your Latin blood, I guess.'

'Why the philosophising, anyway?'

'Just something my crazy sister said. I hope we haven't quarrelled, though. I need her to babysit till you get back on PTA nights till the end of term.'

They have not quarrelled, it transpires. Peaches continues to stop by after work on the requisite evenings until the end of term. Then she disappears on an extended Mediterranean holiday which evidently suits her. When Peaches returns in early autumn she is tanned and blooming.

Jane spots her sister shopping in town, sees her striding slowly with a seraphic smile and fecund glow which suggests Peaches has after all achieved her latest ambition.

'She'll find it harder than she thinks, if she is,' says Jane to Paul as they wait in the cashpoint queue outside the bank while Dario gently kicks his whining brother's ankles.

'Is what?' Paul says. It is his turn now to feed in their plastic card.

'I think Peaches is pregnant.' Jane tries to hiss the P words quietly. The twins hear instantly but Paul is ignoring her, staring curiously at the scarlet digits on the cashpoint display. He has a strange abstracted look on his face, like a man who suddenly realises his account has gained a thousand pounds and hardly dares to wonder how.

MAIRÉAD BYRNE

Hospital room

I did not love them and they did not love me.
They came to visit in the afternoon
during working hours. I was their boss, or at least
the boss of two; the third would get my job.
They brought flowers, stood as if before a firing squad,
and then began to chat, amongst themselves mainly,
sometimes to me, though I could cough
to stave them off, looked pained, gesture to my throat.
When one left, returned with swollen eyes,
I guessed this was the room in which her mother
died. Her cancer far outweighed my tonsillectomy.
A small woman dwindling, becoming minuscule until
I cupped her in my body. She cradled me.
Then they had gone, leaving their noncommittal flowers
on the bed. Bought with petty cash I thought, and since
have thought when looking back. Better to watch sun
fall across a tired coverlet. Better an empty room.

The doctor makes my neighbourhood grow strange

I had laid the poems on Federico García Lorca
on the desk and our eyes met there on the cover,
bashfully. He asked routine questions and I hid
the Band-Aids on my wrists. Then he said,
'Do you hear voices?' And I laughed.
Of course I hear voices, that's it, I hear voices!
I am the book vibrating at the corner of the desk.
I am the desk, I am that doctor and his chalky cheek,
I am his tired mouth, detonations of dust in the air.
I am the photos of his wife and kids, I am his certificates.
I am the garden opening at his back. I am the girl in the glass.
But no, I swung my head slowly from side to side
(which means yes in Turkish) and found myself smartly
marched out the door, prescription in hand, which I filled
when I bowled down the hill to the chemists.
Then on, past Macker's, McHughes, and into
the bone-shaped park to see Mother.
I stood in the rooms listening. Nobody's home.
Then took a clear tumbler of water, the pills.
And soon there I was, knee-deep in traffic and marvelling:
here come the pretty buses, there go the cars.

An interview with
Romulus and Remus

What did you think of the wolves?
Did they excite you?
Make you feel different? More human?
What is it like to be twins?
Did the wolves smell?
Did you find that in any way off-putting?
Did you have trouble expressing affection?
What's wolf's milk like for starters?
What were their names?
Where did they go on their holidays?
Did you find it hard to settle down again in Rome?
We call it Rome now.
I don't mean to cause a fight
but did it ever strike you that Reme
might have been an equally good name?
How do you boys get along?
Was it dark out there? And cold?
Are you glad to be home and how
do you get along with women, real women?
I mean, do they compare to the wolves?
Do you think your background will cause problems later in life?
I mean sexually.
Did you ever have it off with a wolf?
You're too young, I guess.
I don't mean to be disrespectful
but, you see, we never heard the full story.

A lot of people wonder about you boys,
being brought up by wolves and all that.
Do you miss them?
Do you know that they're nearly extinct?
Would you let your daughter marry a wolf?
How fast can you run?
Say, what's your favourite food?
Do you eat raw meat and tear it apart with your teeth?
Well, I suppose that was quite common in Rome.
Hey, thanks for your time, boys.
It's been real.
You gotta learn to talk soon, boys.
A lotta people are dying to hear about this.

Briathra comonta sa teangal/*common verbs in the language*: smiodar/*fragment*

Adhlacaim I bury

Adhmhaim I admit

Agraim I avenge

Aimsim I aim

Ainmnim I name

Aiséirim I rise again

Aistrim I change, translate

Aithrisim I recite, imitate

Athbheoim I revive

Atógaim I reconstruct

Athscríobhhaim I rewrite

Bailim I gather

Baistim I baptise

Beannaim I bless

Beathaim I feed

Beoim I quicken

Blím I milk

Bogaim I loosen, soften

Bronnaim I bestow

Buaim I win

Caillim I lose

Cainin I abuse

Canaim I sing
Caoinim I weep
Casaim I turn, twist
Ceanglaim I fasten, tie
Céilim I conceal
Ciontaim I convict
Clisim I fail
Clóim I overcome
Clúdaim I cover
Cnagaim I strike
Cnuasaim I gather
Coimeadaim I keep
Coisricim I bless
Cosnaim I defend
Cothaim I feed
Cráim I torment
Creidim I believe
Crithim I tremble
Crochaim I hang
Croithim I shake
Cruaim I harden
Crúim I milk
Cruinnim I gather
Cuimhnim I remember
Cumaim I compose, shape

Dearbhaim I swear
Deimhnim I affirm
Díbrim I banish
Dírim I aim
Diultaim I refuse

Dóim I burn
Doirtim I pour out
Dreoim I wither, rot

Éagaim I die
Éalaim I escape
Eirim I rise
Eitlim I fly

Fágaim I leave
Fánaim I stay
Fíafraim I ask
Fillim I return
Fíosraim I inquire
Foghlaimim I learn
Freastalaim I wait upon

Geallaim I propose
Géillim I submit
Glacaim I accept
Glaoim I shout out
Gléasaim I harness
Goidim I steal
Goinim I wound
Goirtim I hurt

Greamaim I grip
Gúim I pray, beseech

Iarraim I ask, seek.

There is no *j* in the Irish language.
There is no *k* in the Irish language.

Leimim I leap

Biographical notes

FERNE ARFIN is an American freelance writer living in London. An actress and former journalist, she is a graduate of Syracuse University and the University of East Anglia, where she studied with Malcolm Bradbury. Her stories have appeared in Bête Noire, Iron, Expo, Writing Women and QWF. She has recently completed a novel and a short film.

ROS BARBER was born in 1964 and is a single mother with three sons. She has twice been commended in the National Poetry Competition, won second prize in the New Writer Poetry Competition in 1997 and has had poems in the Faber Hard Lines 3. She works as a part-time creative writing tutor for the University of Sussex.

ANNA BLACK was born in 1964, has lived in London for the past fifteen years and is currently a commissioning editor for a non-fiction illustrated book list. She started writing about five years ago and her first story was shortlisted for the 1997 Ian St James award.

MAIRÉAD BYRNE was born in Dublin in 1957 and now teaches English at Ithaca College, New York. She was a journalist for seven years and has also written two plays which were produced by the Project Arts Centre in Dublin, a book on James Joyce and two books of interviews with Irish painters. She has published poetry in journals in the USA, Ireland and Britain. She is currently writing a book on childbirth and metaphor.

CATHERINE CONZATO grew up in Sydney, Australia. She moved

to Paris and Milan to work and study languages. She worked in the EU Delegation in Mogadishu before civil war destroyed the city. After brief spells in northern Italy and Brussels she returned to Africa and has lived in Ghana for the past five years. She works with an Accra-based advertising agency and has published stories in Britain, the USA and Australia.

HELEN FARISH was born in 1962 in Cumbria and studied at Durham University. She has recently completed an MA in contemporary poetry. She spent six years working abroad and is now employed as an editor by Oxford University Press. Her poems have appeared in many magazines including PN *Review*, *The Rialto*, *Writing Women*, *London Magazine* and *Stand*. She was awarded a Hawthornden fellowship in 1997.

KATHERINE FROST studied psychology at Oxford and lives in London. Her poems have appeared in *Poetry Review*, *Smiths Knoll*, *The North* and *Poetry London Newsletter*. She divides her time between writing and working as a psychologist. In 1994 she was the overall winner of the Poetry Business Competition. A pamphlet, *The Sixth Channel*, was published by Smith/Doorstop in 1995.

MELANIE GILES grew up in Dorset but has settled in Sheffield. She is a prehistoric archaeologist and is currently in the middle of a Ph.D. Her desire both as an archaeologist and as a writer is to understand and convey the inhabitation of landscape, past and present. The other main concern in her writing is exploration of her twinship with her sister Katherine. Her work has never been published before.

ALYSON HALLETT is a full-time writer who lives in Bristol. She has held many writer-in-residence posts in the south-west and has written text for collaborative performance, installation and an artist's book. She teaches creative writing and is currently working on a novel. Future plans include writing a radio play and an excursion to New Mexico.

SARAH VAN HOVE was born in Bristol in 1959. She read peace studies at Bradford University and has worked in a nursery school in Andhra Pradesh and in a hostel for the homeless. She has also taught English to Asian women. Living in Brussels for the last fifteen years, she has learned Flemish and brought up three children. She now writes full time and is currently working on a novel.

ABI HUGHES-EDWARDS was born in 1961. She has had work published in *Envoi, The Rialto, Staple,* etc. She was a *One Voice* monologue competition winner in 1993 and has had work commissioned by HTV and published by Gomer Press. She is currently poetry editor for *The New Writer.* She likes the sea, gardening, her poodle Gertrude and the artist she lives with.

JEHANE MARKHAM was born in Sussex in 1949 and studied painting at the Central School of Art. She began writing for BBC Radio in the 1970s. Recently she adapted the myth of Cupid and Psyche for Wonderful Beast Theatre Company. She is currently taking a combined degree in film studies and Irish studies and lives in London with her partner and three children.

BARBARA MARSHALL lives in Brighton and works as a teacher of English literature and women's studies. She has published texts about literature for students. She is a poet as well as a short story writer and one of her stories has previously appeared in *Writing Women.*

MARION MATHIEU was born in 1951 in Amityville, Long Island and educated at the Art Student League. She moved to Dublin in 1979 and since 1982 has lived in Northamptonshire where she works as a painter. Her writing has been widely published in magazines including *The New Writer.* She won the Jackson's Arm Poetry Pamphlet award in 1995 and an East Midlands Arts writer's bursary in 1997.

CRYSSE MORRISON is a freelance writer, originally from London but now living in Somerset. She writes for First Cut Theatre Company and has published short stories in many magazines, including *Writing Women*. Her radio play *Feathers* was broadcast in 1997 and her first novel, *Frozen Summer*, is forthcoming from Hodder.

KERRY-LEE POWELL was born in Montreal, Canada in 1969 and has lived in Antigua, Australia and Wales. Her stories and poems have appeared in various magazines. She has just completed her first novel, *Kindness*, a book about Elvis impersonators, transsexuals, love and mothers. She now lives in London with performance artist Paul Granjon and is writing a second novel about born-again Christians, St Augustine, teenage runaways and a mother who falls in love with a social services building.

MARLYNN ROSARIO was born in 1950 and works as a teacher in Newcastle upon Tyne. She recently completed an MA in creative writing at the University of Northumbria and won the Bloodaxe Poetry Prize. Her work has appeared in many magazines, including *London Magazine, Iron* and *Orbis*. She was a prizewinner in the 1997 Poetry Business Competition and has had a pamphlet published by Smith/Doorstop.

PENNY SIMPSON is a director of Earthfall, a dance theatre company. She is a former Theatre Management Association Critic of the Year and recently received an Arts Council bursary to write a first novel. Her short stories have been published in *IoS 1 Anthology* (Bloomsbury, 1997), *Bridport Prize Winners Anthology* and *World Wide Writers 5*.

ALYSS THOMAS was born in 1957, lives in Devon and works as a psychotherapist. She is currently completing an MA in creative writing at the University of Plymouth. She has been published in *North* and *Swimming in the Long Dark Sound*, a Stride Press Publication. Her work was highly commended in the New Writer competition and she is a member of Something Frightening, a women's poetry and performance group.

JESSICA TREAT was born in Canada and now lives in a small town in New York State. Her first story collection – A *Robber in the House* – was published by Coffee House Press in 1993. Her fiction has appeared in many magazines and is included in two recent anthologies, *Chick Lit 2* and *An Intricate Weave*. She received a Dominion Review fiction award in 1996.

SUE VICKERMAN has spent time in rural India, upstate New York, Hangzhou and Berlin. She completed an M.Phil. about spirituality and published a few articles in the national press before writing short stories, poetry and a novel. She now lives in the shadow of the Brontës in Haworth, Yorkshire.

FIONA RITCHIE WALKER was born in Montrose, Scotland in 1956 and now lives in Northumberland. A trained journalist, she has been a charity press officer and a team leader of voluntary construction workers in the Canadian Arctic. Her writing has won prizes in several competitions and has been broadcast on BBC Radio Scotland. She is the wife of a Methodist minister and mother of two boys.

CARMEN WALTON lives in Ashton-under-Lyne and is a freelance writer. She tours with Say So Performance Poets and has broadcast a series of poems on Radio 1, local radio stations and Granada TV. Her stories and poems have appeared in many magazines and anthologies. She has received several awards and bursaries and also teaches creative writing.

LYNN WALTON was born in 1957 and brought up in Whitefield. She now lives in Manchester and has three children. She has worked as an infant teacher. Her interests include horror, science fiction, fantasy and vampires. She has had work published by the Beehive Press and also in the Crocus publication, *Nailing Colours*.